BROKEN WITCH

BROKEN PEAK PACK
BOOK 6

BY JULES CRISARE

BROKEN PEAK PACK

Broken Hero
Broken Sage
Broken Mage
Broken Rebel
Broken Crown
Broken Witch

HIDDEN RUNAWAYS

Hidden Trouble

BLACK HILLS VENDETTA

Wolf's Retribution
Wolf's Revenge
Wolf's Reckoning *(coming to Kickstarter in 2024)*

BOX SETS

Broken Peak Pack eBook Bundle Volume 1
Broken Peak Pack eBook Bundle Volume 2
Broken Peak Pack Omnibus Collector's Edition *(Kickstarter Exclusive)*

SILVER SENTINEL NOVELS

Destined Heir
The Last Immortal Mystery Files *(coming to Kickstarter in 2023)*

SENTINELS OF THE SILVER ORB

BROKEN WITCH

BROKEN PEAK PACK
BOOK 6

BY JULES CRISARE

SILVER ORB BOOKS

BROKEN WITCH

Designed by J. Crisare

0123pbk

ISBN: 978-1-948603-31-7 (pbk.)

A NOTE FROM JULES

Parts of *Broken Witch* take place during *Broken Crown*. While it should be possible to read Broken Witch without having read any other book from the Broken Peak Pack series, I recommend reading *Broken Crown* first for a more enjoyable reading experience.

To my niece who is becoming a young woman I couldn't be more proud of.

PROLOGUE

RING. Sybil looked up from the open book laid out on the kitchen table and glared at the phone for interrupting her reading. The small printing on the vellum pages was hard enough to read without the annoyances of distracting noises.

Ring.

Sybil's eyes narrowed at the avocado green plastic contraption hanging from the wall.

Ri-

A few muttered words and a wave of her hand cut the ring off, and she returned to staring at the wavy line creeping across the pages.

Ring.

Sybil lifted her head and stared at the phone. It dared to disobey the simple command to remain silent.

Ring.

Only one creature could overrule Sybil's order. She'd done her best to avoid any dealings with the said creature, but destiny and fate and magic conspired against her.

Ring.

"Fine. I got your message. I'm coming." Sybil pushed her chair away from the table and slowly rose. Her old bones weren't what they used to be, and she wasn't stupid enough to mess with a magic that might have slowed the aging process.

As though the phone heard her, it stopped its shrill noise. But as soon as her hand hovered over the handset, the phone rang again.

She picked it up and pressed it to her ear. "Yes?"

"It's time." The pleasant, deep voice of an overly confident man came from across the line.

Except the voice didn't belong to a man. It belonged to the last immortal. A creature so powerful that few who lived within the world of magic and the supernatural knew of his existence.

"So soon?"

"They're waiting on the final piece, now."

"She won't be happy." Sybil looked down at the large puppy who followed her from the table to the phone, hopeful for a treat from the jar that sat on the small square counter below the phone.

"None of them were at first."

"I told her everything. It's nothing like the others."

"Sybil..." The male was losing patience.

"Alexander, are you certain? I've been looking at the book and there are warnings about sending her too soon."

"The Hero and Crown are finally together, it's only a matter of time. We need the Witch in place or all of the work I've done over the centuries will be for nothing."

Sybil sighed. She knew the day would come when she'd have to send her granddaughter away. She hoped it was further in the future. Like years away.

Alexander first visited her after her daughter was born. He peered into her newborn daughter's crib and studied the infant for several minutes before declaring she wasn't the one. Sybil had sighed in relief at the pronouncement. Except the relief was short-lived. With the next breath, if the male even breathed air, he declared her granddaughter would likely be the one.

As soon as her daughter turned thirteen and noticed boys for the first time, Sybil did her best to keep her daughter away from any man. She failed in keeping her daughter cloistered away, although that was only because her husband, God rest his soul, had refused to allow Sybil to send their daughter to a nunnery.

And then Cassandra was born. And Alexander visited again. Only this time he didn't peer inside the crib. He knocked on her door and when Sybil opened the door, Alexander simply nodded once.

Since then, he called every few years to check on Cassandra's progress. If Alexander hadn't been around to anoint the Witch, Cassandra's ability to harness the powers that flowed around the Earth would have been enough to alert Sybil.

"What happened to free-will?"

"They all have a choice. If she wants to walk away after she's met with them and spoken with the coyote, no one will stop her."

Sybil rolled her eyes, even if Alexander couldn't see her. Of course, he'd pull out the coyote card.

To help alleviate some of the anxiety caused by sending her granddaughter into a known shifter den, Sybil visited Broken Peak. Annnnd she might have struck up a teensy relationship with the coyote. Sybil hadn't actually met the male, but she had spent time with the animal.

Not as a woman, though. That went without saying. She had borrowed the body of a local badger, and might have continued to visit after that first time. Hey, life as a widower in a small seaside town in New Hampshire got boring.

"Sybil, the Hero isn't the only one who will need the help of a Voisin." Alexander chuckled, as though he was enjoying a joke only he found amusing. "Why don't you pack a bag for yourself too."

"Fine." Well, wasn't that fantastic. She knew her visits to the coyote would come back to bite her on the ass at some point.

"I'm not sure it's best for you to travel with your granddaughter, Sybil."

"Please, I'm not an idiot, Alexander." Sybil rolled her eyes again. "I've read the same words you have. She has to make this journey on her own. Without my help."

"Sybil?" The male's voice turned smooth and charming again.

"What, Alexander?" She had enough of the conversation, and of Alexander du Mabillion.

"Give Cassandra a few weeks to settle in before coming to War. Oh, and when you come down, bring your books with you."

Sybil didn't respond. She hung up the phone before Alexander could offer any more of his suggestions. Too bad none of the Voisin line had the gift of prophecy or maybe they would have joined the Concord if it meant anyone other than du Mabillion was selected.

Except there was a very good reason the Voisin line refused to join the Concord all those generations ago. It was the same reason Cassandra was going to be headed to War, West Virginia. A vow made centuries ago to the Great Shifters. They would ensure the survival of the Voisin line through the generations until one of the Voisin women would return the favor and ensure the survival of the Great Shifter when the time came.

Sybil reached into the ceramic jar on the counter and handed Moose a dog treat. "She's gonna be angry, Moose. Don't let her get too angry at me."

The border collie lab cross looked up at her with soulful brown eyes and gave her a vigorous wag of his white-tipped tail.

"And keep her safe until I get down there." She gave him another treat.

And Moose gave her another wag of his tail.

CHAPTER ONE

CASSANDRA Voisin pounded her palm against the front door of her grandmother's farmhouse. Not that it would do any good. Once her grandmother had made up her mind about anything, she never changed it. Ever. Memaw wanted Cassandra to head south to some Podunk village in the middle of absolutely nowhere and fulfill some stupid ass promise some ancestor supposedly made to a creature that never existed except in children's books. Why? Because the Voisin's did not, under no circumstances whatsoever, break a promise. Even one made thousands of years ago.

But the problem with the whole promise thing is that one had to believe in a few premises that were faulty to begin with. The first was that as far as Cassandra knew, griffins and dragons did not exist and never existed. Unless someone somewhere confused a dinosaur with a dragon, but then dinosaurs had to exist when humans did, which they didn't. The second was the idea that one of Cassandra's ancestors, made a promise to said fanciful creature over two thousand years ago, closer to three if family legend was anything to go by, but the same family legend said dragons and griffins existed, so Cassandra didn't give it much credence, and each generation handed down that promise the next generation. Except, anyone with a tiny bit of understanding how family trees worked could safely assume that most everyone and their mother were beholden to that same promise.

And if that was the case, then Cassandra didn't need to go to the Podunk village in West Virginia because a half a million other people would make the same trip. That was if Cassandra accepted a promise had been made and dragons and griffins existed.

Which they didn't.

Then again, nothing about Cassandra's life could have been considered normal by any rational measure. She was a witch, after all. No, not the kind of witch that worshiped nature, though she did in a way, but the honest-to-goodness kind of witch who could cast spells. Yeah, the people who believed they were witches cast the same spells sometimes, but most lacked the bit of power wrestled from nature to ensure the casting was true.

Cassandra had never actually tried to ride a broom, but with the right spell and the perfect pinch of power, she could probably fly one across the sky on Halloween for shits and giggles. Although, according to family legend, Cassandra's mother made the Electrolux hover three feet in the air while straddling the canister when she was four. That was the moment when Memaw made the executive decision that from that point on all Voisin women needed to be home schooled. It was also how Memaw determined, arbitrarily, if anyone had bothered to ask

Cassandra her opinion, that if her daughter wasn't the one destined to keep the promise, then it would be her granddaughter.

Cassandra was regretting her Memaw's decision.

"Come on, Memaw! Let me in! The neighbors already think we're kooky enough without you locking me out of the house!"

Wait, the back door.

Cassandra high-kneed it around the small farmhouse to the back door, but it was locked up tight. Like the front door. She stepped back and stared up at the second-floor windows. No way the old bat could get up the stairs and lock all the windows. And just because Cassandra hadn't tried the flying thing before didn't mean she couldn't fly.

Right?

She gnawed on her bottom lip and side-eyed the neighbors to her right. Sure, they lived about a quarter mile away, but it would be her luck that they were out and about right at the moment she took to the air.

A high-pitched whine came from inside the house, immediately followed by the thump of an eighty pound dog throwing himself against the window.

Moose had serious issues, including a severe case of co-dependency and did not, under any circumstance, like it when Cassandra was not within his immediate sight. She couldn't close the door to the bathroom without him throwing a fit. It was a wonder the windows were still in place, considering he pounded on them with his front paws when she walked down the driveway to get the mail. And that was when she was gone for less than a minute. Imagining the beating those windows took when she was gone for an hour bordered on terrifying.

A door slammed closed and the jingle jangle of Moose's collar announced his impending arrival, which included much barking and jumping.

"You saw me less than five minutes ago."

Moose wiggled in response.

A window on the second floor opened and Memaw poked her head out. "It's a fourteen-hour trip. The sooner you leave, the better."

"I am not going." For good measure, Cassandra stomped her foot. "I don't have a bag packed or anything.

Memaw's head disappeared and an over-stuffed duffel bag appeared. As soon as the bag landed on the snow-covered ground in front of Cassandra, the window slammed closed.

The old coot had an answer for everything.

"What about Moose's food?" Cassandra yelled.

Another door slam.

This was so not happening. Cassandra pressed the heels of her palms against her eyes and shook her head.

Except it was. All the power she could harness wouldn't get her out of the mess some idiot of an ancestor and her gullible grandmother had gotten her into.

Cassandra grabbed the duffel, which almost knocked her over as she slung it over her shoulder. "Sheesh, Memaw. What did you pack in here?" She didn't want to know. Sometimes not knowing was better than knowing, and Cassandra was fairly sure that this was one of those occasions. "Come on, Moose. I guess it's you and me."

She trudged around the house through the few inches of snow to the detached garage with an eighty-pound dog hopping for joy around her feet at the prospect of going for a car ride. Yeah, this was going to be a funnnnn trip. Maybe if she added more N's to it, she might actually believe it.

The garage was more of a barn than a garage and didn't have an automatic door, so Cassandra set the bag down and performed a healthy squat to get the door up without wrenching her back. She even reiterated the whole *lift with her legs* mantra in her mind. Sure, she could have used her magic to help, but this was one of those times when she wasn't a hundred percent sure using magic wouldn't fall completely on the selfish side of the scale.

The first lesson Memaw and her mother taught Cassandra was that any magic performed under a selfish motivation would backfire and cause more problems than doing the task without magic would have.

She'd never actually tested it out. The stories of the catastrophic chains of events had been enough to frighten her away from using magic for tasks she could just as easily complete by hand.

"I am so killing Memaw when we get back, Moose."

Moose grunted back at her. Of course, he did. The little traitor loved Memaw almost as much as he loved Cassandra, but that was because Memaw fed him treats all day long.

A 1962 Plymouth Valiant, painted in the same sun-glo yellow as when it had been first purchased brand new off the lot, stood next to the land yacht. Memaw couldn't stomach selling the Valiant, but every few years she traded in her Lincoln Continental for a new model. The old bat didn't put more than a few thousand miles on her vehicles, but she insisted on trading them in, nonetheless.

Cassandra had no idea what Memaw was going to do the next time she went to trade in her car, since Lincoln recently discontinued the Continental. As Cassandra tossed one of the bags into the back seat, she grinned. Not because she was happy to be driving anywhere, but because it served Memaw right. If she wanted to stick with a Lincoln, then Memaw would be driving an SUV or a Continental that was older than two years old.

Once she arranged their bags into neat stacks in the back of the Valiant, Cassandra let Moose get into the car. She'd tried to give him the entire back seat before, but he insisted on riding in the front seat next to her. The little fiend was over eighty pounds, but managed to curl up into a tight ball and fit into the front seat without any appendages dangling off the edges. Why he couldn't do that everywhere else, Cassandra hadn't figured out. And she had spent more time contemplating that particular question than she cared to admit.

The car started easily, and as she backed it out of the garage, she sent a word of thanks to the little bits of magic hovering around the older vehicle. Memaw instilled Cassandra with a healthy amount of respect for the powers that flittered around and made the Voisin women's lives a little easier. As long as the motivation wasn't purely selfish, the magic never backfired. And that magic was the only reason the Valiant still moved. Well, magic and the twice a year checkups with a local mechanic.

Once clear of the garage, Cassandra hopped out of the car and pulled the mammoth door back down. By the time she got back into the car, Moose was sitting behind the steering wheel.

"Trust me, if you could drive, I'd let you. Now scoot over." She slid into the seat and pushed the dog over. Who wasn't certain what was going on, but didn't want to be left out of the action.

Cassandra drove her car along the highway, counting the exits down until her destination. They'd stopped at a hotel off the side of the highway before leaving Pennsylvania. The hope had been to reach Maryland before stopping for the night, but Cassandra gave that wish up as a pipe dream. As well as finding a hotel room filled with modern amenities and belonging to a national chain, preferably one beginning with an 'H', ending with an 'N', and 'ilto' in the middle.

Instead, she found a bed-and-breakfast named The Old Jail. Hopefully it didn't have any bars on the windows.

It was either the bed-and-breakfast or renting out a mansion. Which, she seriously considered, except she'd need to use magic, and that bordered too closely on the selfish side of the scale.

According to the directions, The Old Jail was in the middle of town and within walking distance to restaurants. It was also at the head of a stretch of highway named the back of the dragon.

But Cassandra chose to ignore that nugget of information because it fed into the stupid legend her grandmother insisted wasn't a legend, but was fact.

The map on her phone alerted her to the approaching exit, which she took. The voice on the phone then gave her turn by turn directions to the large red brick building. She pulled into the parking lot and put the Valiant into park, but didn't turn the car off. Turning off the ignition was one step too close to admitting she bought into one of her ancestors making a promise to a mythological creature a few thousand years ago.

That assumed she trusted the math skills of a crazy ancestor.

What was she doing here?

At any point during the fourteen hours driving, she could have turned around or headed in any other direction away from War. She had a choice. Her memaw and the big book of witchy things might disagree, but free will still existed.

Tomorrow she would get back in her car and drive west into the sunset. Except she'd leave well before the sun set.

Cassandra snapped the leash on Moose's collar, grabbed her phone and purse, and got both of them out of the car without anyone falling over. Moose stretched out his hind legs before finding a perfect spot to pee, while Cassandra shifted her weight from foot to foot and waited.

Well, at least there was a silver lining. It was January and no snow. New Hampshire was still in the middle of snow season, but War only had brown grass.

"Come on, Moo, let's get our room then go for a walk and grab some dinner."

CHAPTER TWO

"**COME** on, Tevin, it's not like you have all that many shirts to choose from." Finley propped up the wall with his shoulder, keeping one eye on his friend and packmate and another eye on the hallway where the rest of his pack danced impatiently.

"Look, you all have your mates. They don't care what you look like. If I want any action, I have to at least look halfway presentable."

"What's taking so long?" Allard, the freshly mated packmate who was the reason for the impromptu visit into town, pushed into Tevin's room. "Oh."

Yeah, oh was right.

Tevin stood in front of the mirror, buttoning up the faded burgundy chambray shirt over a clean t-shirt, thanks to Eleanor, Jackson's mate and the only reason anyone had clean clothes.

The first member of Broken Peak Pack, after Bray, their Alpha, was also the youngest. And he had never, not in all the years since Finley had known him, spent any time picking out his clothes. Hell, there was a time when Tevin refused to wear any clothes at all because they'd been hand-me-downs from his older packmates.

While the current version of Tevin was an improvement from the nudist version, it didn't matter to the others, who were waiting impatiently before heading down to the garage. Where, if pack history was anything to go by, everyone would argue over who got to drive and who sat where. Which, by Finley's estimation, would end up adding another forty minutes to their estimated time of departure.

"I'll wait for the clothes horse here. You go on and get the others to the garage, and watch Maggie for me, would you? Delia gave her a purse and it's anyone's guess what might end up inside it." The last thing Finley, or any of the pack, needed was for his mate with the sticky fingers to stash a weapon inside the purse because it seemed like a good idea at the time.

"I think it just has chapstick in it, but I'll give it a search before I let her in the car." Allard smirked at Finley, gave Tevin a shake of his head, and left the room to herd the others down to the garage.

"You could have gone with them."

Tevin unbuttoned his shirt and reached for another button down, this one pale green. Or maybe it was turquoise. Finley didn't care much about colors that fell outside the seven major ones that made up the rainbow. A quick glance at Tevin's closet revealed a lot more clothes than Finley remembered Tevin having.

"Where did you get all these?"

"If you ask Vixen nicely, she'll add on shit you need when she does her ordering thing."

"You trust Vixen's judgment when it comes to clothes?" After the Halloween fiasco, when Bray's mate and the second Alpha of their pack, Vixen, dressed them up as The Village People, Finley avoided letting her anywhere near his wardrobe. Not that he needed anything more than shirts and jeans, and as long as they fit, he didn't care much what they looked like.

"Shit no. I give her a list of what I want, and she tacks them on to her orders."

Finley shrugged. "Not sure she's the best one to ask anymore. Vixen's been preoccupied with that fucking mumbo jumbo. Last time I made a request for some new underwear, I got a grown up version of Underoos. Did you know they made that shit for grown ass men? I wanted boxer briefs and instead got a pair of He-Man Underoos. They come with brown briefs, Tevin. Who the fuck wants to wear brown underwear?"

The fucking mumbo jumbo was actually recently discovered entries in the journals written by one of Mac's ancestors. If the entries were anything to go by, she was certifiably crazy. Hell, they didn't need to go by the journals. Mac was an old coyote shifter who more than likely inherited his ancestor's crazy. After all, it was his bright idea for Bray to claim Vixen, which unlocked the griffin who was kind of sleeping inside Vixen.

"Well, Costco has some cool things sometimes. Which you'd know if you ever spent any time away from Maggie and did the grocery run with Vixen or Bray."

"You know I can't make a Costco run anymore. Someone has to keep Maggie distracted, or she insists on going. And then we have a repeat of the time I had to pick them up because they bought enough crap to fill not one, but two of the Expeditions."

Tevin paused in buttoning up his shirt, and stared at Finley. He wasn't buying it. Neither was Finley, but it sounded good in his brain before he actually said the words out loud.

"Go ahead with the others, I'll meet up with you." Tevin ran a brush through his hair and checked his breath in his hand.

"What the hell is wrong with you?" Finley asked. "Do I need to check under your bed for a pod or something?"

The male standing in front of him was nothing like the male he remembered. Tevin had always been the annoying packmate who didn't give a fuck about anything.

"Seriously, Fin?" Tevin brushed Finley aside and stomped his way out of the room and down the hallway. "I'm not a pup anymore."

"You still write your name on shit. You wrote your name on the soap."

"That's because it's soap and I don't want to use the same soap you used to clean your dick and balls."

Finley hurried after him. Tevin had a point, but he didn't want to think too much about the subject of where the soap had been.

"Maggie's special, yeah?"

"Hm?" Finley was still not thinking about where the soap had been.

"Your mate, Maggie? She's special, right?"

"Damn straight she is."

Finley wasn't sure how he convinced her to stay when she was ready to run, but the little raccoon shifter not only rocked his world, but the pack's world as well. Most shifters tended to mate with their own kind, but Broken Peak didn't follow any of the traditions. The only thing that mattered when it came to Maggie was that she was Finley's mate. End of discussion. But Finley didn't think Tevin was asking about the politics of Maggie being a raccoon shifter and living with a pack of wolf shifters.

"I can't decide if you're unlucky or lucky, but I'm leaning towards lucky."

"Why do you say that?"

"You found your mate. Hell, even Allard found his, with the female he was supposed to mate. If that's not luck, then I don't know what it is."

Finley grinned and bobbed his head up and down. Yeah, he did find his mate, but it was more of his mate finding him. Shit, in Allard's case, Delia found him.

But Tevin had always avoided spending more time than necessary with the mates. Except for Maggie. And that was probably more about Maggie and less about Tevin. The last member of their pack that Finley ever thought would find a mate, much less want to find a mate, was Tevin. Hell, before Vixen's arrival and the security lock-down, Tevin spent more time in town at the bars than anyone else. He spent as many nights in his own bed as he did in another's.

Well, no, that wasn't necessarily true. He never actually spent the night in anyone else's bed.

"A mate would cramp your style, Tev." Finley winked at his pack-mate. "You wouldn't be able to slip out in the middle of the night to get back to your own bed."

Tevin stared straight ahead, avoiding Finley's comment. "Who says what my style is?"

Well, shit. Maybe they had it all wrong. "Look, Tev-"

"Whatever, man, no worries." He looked back up at Finley with a smirk and hurried out the lodge and toward the path that would lead them to the massive garage that held the pack's vehicles. "Come on, they're waiting for us. Right?"

CHAPTER THREE

"YOU'RE sure about this?"

Max stretched out on the bed in a local inn and folded his arms behind his head while ignoring his colleagues' questions. Given the opportunity, he would have taken the job on his own, without Tweedledee and Tweedledumber. Alas, that wasn't an option and so now he had to contend with two half-wits who would just make the job more difficult.

They recently joined the Black Hills Pack, and this was their chance to prove themselves, but they'd been one fuck-up after another. From losing the female on the road when Max had grabbed less than twenty minutes of sleep. How the fuck did anyone lose a high-end Mercedes with Illinois plates on a highway through the middle of fucking nowhere? To the whole questioning everything Max ordered.

What was Seth thinking? As the leader of Black Hills, he should never have accepted the idiot twins into the fold. If Max had been the leader, and if you asked him, he should have been, no way would he let in half the shifters who showed up at the door. But Seth had a soft spot for second sons of Alphas and never asked questions.

"Seriously, Max, are you-"

"Yes, I'm sure." He cut off Tweedledee, or was it Tweedledum? Not that it mattered who said what. The idiot twins were interchangeable in Max's mind. With a sigh, he slid off the bed and headed to the bathroom. Maybe a few minutes of peace and quiet in the shower would settle some of his nerves and lower the risk of killing the idiot twins.

"But Seth said to stay out of sight."

"Thanks for the news flash."

Seth had definitely ordered them to stay out of sight, but the leader of the Black Hills Pack didn't have the first clue what awaited them in Broken Peak. When they first arrived, Max had scouted the area and learned what awaited them if they had to snatch the female inside pack territory.

No way would the Alphas of Broken Peak let anyone walk away unscathed. If they wanted any chance of success, they needed to catch Delia while she was in town and far away from the watchful eye of that fucking Alpha female.

"Don't worry about the change of plans. I'll handle it with Seth." Max stepped into the bathroom and closed the door behind him. Shutting down the inevitable protests before they began.

"Why don't we call him?"

"I'll take care of it." Max growled low and his wolf pushed towards the surface. He banged the back of his head against the bathroom door and closed his eyes while counting to ten.

Just like I'm taking care of a lot of things Max thought as he considered what he was doing in War.

Their budget didn't allow them more than one room at the one nice hotel, and finding privacy was damn near impossible. Most of War consisted of houses barely able to call themselves houses, a string of dive bars, and businesses barely hanging on and The Old Jail was the nicest hotel in town. The owner wasn't a local, but he made a few appearances from what Max had heard.

Not that it mattered, though. Max couldn't care less about the owner as long as the owner wasn't a shifter.

He pulled out the burner phone that his contact mailed him when Seth sent them out on this stupid assignment.

The phone was an old flip style and made texting nearly impossible with having to push numbers as many as three times, but it was the most secure way for Max to communicate with his contact.

A few more extra jobs and then Max would have enough money to start his own pack. One similar to the Black Hills Pack, but they would take all the jobs offered if the money was right. Maybe, if Max played his cards right, he'd take over the Black Hills Pack. But that was still a ways away, and he needed to get through this job before he made any plans.

Max flipped the phone open and stared at the screen.

He sent a quick text to his contact. *I'm available.*

The contact was from some small pack in the southeast whose pack didn't have any real power. Like Max, he came from a small pack and didn't have a future. Not because the pack didn't have a healthy bank account to support it, but because packs were ingrained in stupid traditions and believed in the stupid stories passed down through the generations.

The phone vibrated in his hand.

Max read the words on the screen.

Status Report.

Nothing changed since the last time his contact asked.

Am I leading this mission?

The phone remained still in Max's hand. After a few minutes, it vibrated, signaling a new message.

In the technical sense, yes.

So, let me take care of things on my end, and I'll let you know when I have an update.

Regular status updates are part of your mission.

Even when nothing's changed?

When we don't hear from you, we worry. You don't want us worried, do you?

Shit, the contact was using "we". That usually meant the Alpha of the small pack was speaking through the contact. He had the patience of a kid on Christmas morning.

Do you want to hear no change every hour? War is a small town, but the target is well-protected. Once we've made contact, I'll advise you.

We're funding this mission.

I know. Max was growing tired of the constant texts, and he was sure his contact was tired of waiting for Max to find a moment in private to respond. *I'll take care of everything.*

Of course, you will.

Max squinted at the screen of the phone. He'd been through these conversations enough with previous solo missions. That a southeast pack had similar interest in the same target as a southwest pack was a happy coincidence. All he could do was wait for a response.

And hope the two idiots outside didn't barge into the bathroom.

You came highly recommended. Did we make a mistake?

There it was. The passive aggressive threat. Of course, they took a passive aggressive approach. They didn't want to get their hands dirty by going after the daughter of the most powerful wolf shifter pack. There was no way they'd be ballsy enough to actually come out and threaten Max.

No wonder their pack was so weak.

Max took his time responding. Partially because he felt his temper rising and his wolf pushing closer to the surface, but mostly because he had to press the same button several times to send the full message.

You hired me and I'll complete the ordered job on my own terms. When we made the agreement, there was no time limit involved. If you now have a deadline, the fee goes up.

The talk of money always ended every difficult conversation, no matter who was on the other end. He'd learned that early on. Max closed the phone and stuck it back into his pocket, then thought better of it. The bathroom had a vent just above the toilet, and it would be the perfect hiding place for the phone in case Tweedledee or Tweedledum decided to come in because they couldn't hold it, or for some other asinine reason.

He pulled out his Leatherman tool and unfastened the screws and popped out the vent cover. Before he put the phone back in its new temporary home, he turned it off. No need to alert anyone with its vibrating. Besides, he didn't need to say anything else to his contact. At least not until the job was done. When he put the cover back into place, Max left the screws out. Those he hid beneath the liner of the garbage can.

Once everything was nice and tidy, he stripped and hopped into the shower. Might as well take advantage of the momentary quiet.

Plus, the idiot twins would probably ask why Max's hair wasn't wet after he spent as much time in the bathroom with the shower running.

CHAPTER FOUR

TEVIN strode into the Dirty Whistle and bit back the urge to groan. The couples surrounding him made the trip to the bar about as thrilling as a root canal. Not that Tevin had ever had a root canal, but he heard about them from others. At least they had gone to a bar, and he could spend the evening drinking.

A lot, if he was going to get through the evening without gagging.

When Allard handed back the beers to the rest of the pack, Tevin snatched two, then headed towards one of the few empty tables in the bar. Not that the Dirty Whistle was known as a sit-down establishment, but they only had a handful of high-tops. That a table was available was a fucking miracle.

Even better, it was in a corner and gave Tevin and the others a clear view of the room and the door.

It didn't take a rocket scientist to figure out something was up. Since Vixen's arrival at Broken Peak, none of the males had ventured to a bar for a relaxing evening in town. Tevin might have sneaked out on a few nights, but that was only after Danielle, Leighton's mate, arrived and added several layers of security to the pack.

"I. Love. Costco!" Maggie jumped around and Tevin looked away from her enthusiasm.

There was only so much of Maggie's unbridled joy that he could take, and no amount of beer in the world could help.

The others shared stories about the pack with Delia, and Tevin finished his first bottle of beer. Yeah, it was definitely going to be a multiple drink night. Maybe he could slip away to the bar and get a shot of something.

But then, alcohol didn't really have the same effect on shifters as it did on humans, and Tevin would need to drink a few bottles of bourbon in less than an hour to get as drunk as he needed to be.

Aw, crap, they were kissing now.

Tevin rubbed the heels of his hand against his eyes, sort of wishing that he could erase the image from his retinas.

Gratefully, Finley intervened. "We need more beer!"

And the new happy couple ventured back to the bar, leaving Tevin to consider how miserable life in the pack would be.

As far as Tevin could tell, he had two options. Stay at Broken Peak and be miserable, or leave and hopefully find a pack who was in need of an Alpha. That was the whole reason he came to Broken Peak to begin with. No Alpha wanted an Alpha in their pack that wasn't their own son.

That was why he was sent away in the first place. After his parents died in a car crash, the Alpha of his pack kicked him out. He wasn't even twelve years old and living on the street. For a year, Tevin did the best he could to survive. The only reason he was still alive and hadn't gone feral was because a female shifter found him and sent him to Mac, who promptly dropped Tevin off at Bray's front door.

As shitty as life was at Broken Peak with all the couples, it was a hell of a lot better than wandering in the world on his own.

Movement in Tevin's peripheral vision yanked him out of his melancholy, and he turned his attention to the man talking with Delia and Allard.

The man was unfamiliar, but he spoke with Allard as though they knew one another.

Tevin narrowed his eyes and took a deep breath. No unfamiliar scents from fur. However, there was a slightly odd scent of magic. And not like the not-human magic that Vixen had. This was old magic.

The last time he remembered smelling old magic in the air was right before the female came and picked him up off the street.

"What is it?" Finley asked.

"Nothing. Just thought I saw someone I recognized."

"Who?" Maggie's head spun around as she scanned the bar, but Finley wrapped his arm around her neck before she drew attention to the rest of the pack standing at the table.

"Don't worry about it, Pocket. This was Tevin's favorite hangout. I'd be surprised if he didn't see someone he knew here."

Tevin kept his gaze locked on the man as he turned away from Allard and Delia and melted into the crowd.

Unfortunately Tevin's excuse didn't prevent the litany of questions the rest of the pack shot out at Delia and Allard as soon as they returned.

When Allard didn't answer any questions about the man with the old Magic and Delia changed the subject, Tevin shifted around the table, so he had a better view of the bar. He wasn't certain why he expected it. Maybe it was his wolf who alerted him, but he wasn't surprised when the bell above the door rang. He was the last of his pack to look at the door.

Three males stood in front of the door and scented the air. Just as the five males from Broken Peak were doing.

"Five to three."

Of course, Leighton would be the one spoiling for a fight. And from the looks of the males, they could handle five males. They probably would lose, but not before inflicting a lot of damage. The best action was not to fight, but explaining that to Leighton would fall on deaf ears.

"Excuse me." The female's voice was deep and husky and sent a tingle down Tevin's spine.

Shit. He hadn't seen her naked body, and he wanted a taste of her.

"I said, excuse me."

The female pushed through the wall of males and emerged on the other side in full view of the entire room.

Fuck him. She looked as good as she sounded. Tall, like really tall, since the top of her head hit somewhere between the males' noses and chins. Her long blond hair fell down past her shoulders. And whad'ya know? Her body was rocking, too. All curves and swells. She looked like she came right out of one of those old movies.

"Didn't your mamas teach you boys any manners?" She didn't wait for a response before sashaying her way through the crowd to the bar. "Sheesh, you'd think you'd been born in a barn."

And just like that, the night turned from a boring love fest into a different kind of love fest. "Am I needed here? Or do you all think you can handle this. Because a woman is standing over at the bar who has my name written all over her."

"Yeah, go for it."

Allard gave Tevin the okay, and he grabbed both his beers then headed toward the delightful woman. "Don't wait for me, I'll make my own way home."

After he spent most of the night with the blond, because there was no way he wouldn't find a way to spend as much time as he could with her.

The way she waved to get the bartender's attention, all bent over the bar with her ass up in the air drove Tevin wild. And then the female had the audacity to kick up a leg, and every man within a ten-foot radius eyed her.

Nope. Wasn't happening. Not if Tevin had anything to do with it.

CHAPTER FIVE

CASSANDRA closed her eyes and let out a long, slow breath as the heat of the bodies pushed against her. Why had Cassandra listened to the suggestion to go out for the evening to a bar? She wasn't a bar type of girl. And she definitely wasn't a dive bar type of girl. Yet here she was, in the middle of what might be the dirtiest bar she'd ever seen, much less stepped inside.

Although, the more she thought about it, she hadn't actually listened to a suggestion. Instead, it was a compulsion. What was weird about the whole thing was that Cassandra hadn't realized it was a compulsion until she stood behind the three shifters blocking the way into the bar. But by then, whatever accompanied the suggestion made it impossible for her to turn away.

Yet, despite her knowing that she wasn't at the Dirty Whistle by her own choice, she was standing in front of the bar in a vain attempt to get the bartender's attention, so she could get a drink and then hopefully head back to the little room at the inn.

Well, one thing was for certain, she would not be visiting the Dirty Whistle again. In fact, she still planned on leaving War the following morning.

After a few minutes of waving and clearing her throat loudly, Cassandra promised herself that she would leave. But she hadn't moved away from the bar and instead leaned forward, making it impossible for the bartender to ignore her.

Finally, the man behind the bar, who either didn't want to be there or didn't want her to be there, stopped in front of her.

"What do you want?"

"Um." Crap. She should have had her order ready to go. A quick survey of the shelf along the back of the bar, and she came to the conclusion the best option was something with the highest alcohol content, except nothing on the top shelf came close to typical top-shelf liquor. She pulled out a ten out of her pocket, handed it to the bartender, and placed her order. "Miller Lite, please."

While she waited for her beer, she turned her back to the bar and leaned her elbows against the counter.

Most of the bar was filled with humans, but beneath all the layers of the mundane lurked a hint of magic. Lots of shifter magic, but that was to be expected with the three males still posturing at the front door. Shifters, she expected. What she didn't expect was the lingering ebbs of old magic twisting around the perimeter of the room.

Cassandra peered around the room, looking for the source of the old magic, and her gaze landed on an approaching male. Shifter, if the magic seeping from him was anything to go by. She couldn't tell what animal he was, not unless she wanted to cast a spell in a crowded bar. Shifters had a magic within them, completely different from the entities who manipulated the magic, and it was simple for Cassandra to spot them.

His dark hair was longer, brushing the collar of his shirt, and in need of a haircut. Stubble graced his jawline, probably from shaving earlier in the day. But his whiskers did little to hide the sharp lines of his jaw and cheeks. The male was beautiful to look at, that was for sure. He also didn't dress like the locals. Sure, he had the worn jeans that hugged the muscles of his legs, but the flannel was missing. In place of the plaid flannel was a pale green button down shirt with a white t-shirt underneath.

Damn, the male was gorgeous.

But his gaze wasn't on Cassandra. He was scanning the entire room, obviously looking for someone. As he moved closer to the bar, the humans nearby stepped away. Most probably didn't realize they were doing it, but everyone deferred to his presence.

That was the thing about shifter magic, no one quite knew how it worked exactly, but humans sensed its power. The feeling of something lurking in the woods? The tingling on the back of the neck? The sense of being watched? That was all shifter magic.

Cassandra didn't know who the male was, not that she made a habit of knowing the details of pack life, but his broodiness bordered on gorgeous. His appearance was like catnip to most women, and he probably had his choice of the few women who were in the bar, even if they came with someone else.

Shit, he probably didn't have to deliver some cheesy pick up line. Instead, he'd lift an eyebrow, or maybe his chin, and the women would come running.

She turned back to the bar and her beer. Once she drank the beer, the compulsion might lift, and she could return to the inn. Plus, it wasn't like it was any of her business who he was looking for.

Except as soon as her fingers wrapped around the chilled bottle, she turned back around to stare at the male. And he stared right back at her. Or maybe he was staring at one of the women in front of her.

Before she embarrassed herself by being caught mid-stare, Cassandra picked up the bottle, brought it to her lips, and drank. She probably should have focused more on drinking and less on not getting caught staring. The beer went down the wrong way, and she ended up getting caught coughing like a fool.

The coughing fit ended after she turned back to face the counter and lifted her arms up over her head. As a result, she made a bigger fool of herself.

A strong hand landed on her back and hip. Cassandra straightened and tried to turn around, but a wall of muscle pressed against her back, keeping her in place. The warmth of his breath flowed across the skin of her neck, and goose bumps accompanied the shiver that raced through her body.

"You okay?" The low, rumbling voice sent another shiver down her spine.

Cassandra couldn't find any words. Which didn't happen very often, but she managed a quick nod.

"You sure?"

"Yeah." Another nod accompanied the scratch of her voice.

The wall of muscle took her at her word and pressed his hips against her ass. Either he had a large cylindrical object in his pocket or an erection.

Holy crap, the male was huge all over.

The only thing keeping Cassandra from driving her elbow into the male's throat was his magic. Her shifter had come to her rescue.

The hand on her back slipped around her waist and pressed her back against him until not a molecule existed between them. She was seconds away from pushing him away when the quiet voice in her head reminded her she didn't want him to stop.

God, was she that horny? She didn't even know his name, or anything about him other than the fact that he was gorgeous, a shifter, and sized proportionally.

He gently pulled her away from the bar, and she didn't stop him. When his lips found her ear, she wished for a kiss. Instead, he did a low whisper growl thing that sent butterflies into a massive acrobatic display.

"Are you adventurous?"

Hell yes, she was adventurous. She drove halfway down the east coast because her grandma told her to.

She turned to answer his question, but his massive body prevented her from moving. The stubble on his jaw tickled her cheek, and he nipped her ear.

Too many sensations invaded her body all at once.

"Your arms are still around me."

"That they are." His low chuckled rolled through him and vibrated against her. "Come back to my table with me?"

A wave of old magic rolled across the bar and along with it came the signature of the compulsion. Cassandra turned her head until she could see the source.

"You! This is all your fault!"

The man looked over at her and grinned. "I know."

Oh, crap on a cracker. The man didn't raise his voice, yet Cassandra heard his words over the crowd's chattering.

The shifter slipped his arm around her shoulder and tucked her against his side. She couldn't say for certain, but she thought she heard him growl. For a moment she looked over at the shifter, now that he wasn't behind her, and didn't have her pinned to his chest.

Yep. Just as she suspected. Even more gorgeous close up.

When Cassandra returned her attention to the source of the old magic, he was gone. And so were the three males by the door. Except she could still sense more shifter magic in the bar, and it wasn't coming from the male next to her.

A shrill whistle pierced the noise of the bar.

"You coming?"

"Nope, I'll see you later." The shifter barely looked away from her. "Join me at the now empty table?"

"Didn't you come with friends?"

Mentioning the friend thing didn't quite work when the person with the friends was the male, but it served its purpose in a roundabout way. By playing the friend card, she let the shifter know she had been seen with him. Except as soon as she spoke the words, she wished she could take them back in case she might have offended him.

"Yeah, but I'm a big boy. I can take care of myself."

Yep, he was definitely big. "Okay then."

"Okay?"

"Okay to being adventurous and going to that table with you."

The male laughed again and the sound rolled through her, sending pleasant waves of warmth along with it. Cassandra stumbled, and the male's arm slipped down around her waist, supporting her as they continued on toward the small table in the corner of the bar, outside the sight of just about everyone. Unless someone was looking, they wouldn't notice the table or anyone standing around it.

He looked over at her with a crooked smile with only one side lifting, and it enhanced the air of sexiness he cultivated.

"I don't know your name." She asked. Although, it wasn't really a question.

"And I don't know yours. So we're even." He answered. But it wasn't really an answer.

"Cassandra."

"I'm Tevin."

"Kevin?" She wasn't sure she heard him right.

"No, Tevin, with a T. But my friends call me Tev."

Wait, did that mean he wanted her to call her Tev? No. Of course not. They weren't friends. They'd only just met, if anyone could call their introduction a meeting. And what did it matter if they were friends or not? She was leaving in the morning. Right?

Cassandra reminded herself that nothing about their meeting was the start of a beautiful and amazing relationship. It wasn't like she was going to call her grandmother and give her a play-by-play of the evening.

It was what it was. An extremely sexy male who invited her to join him alone at a table. And since she was planning on leaving, there would be no last names, no strings, and no future.

CHAPTER SIX

THE last place Cassandra belonged was the Dirty Whistle. Tevin could picture her sitting in a small restaurant. The kind with tablecloths and different kinds of waiters. Hell, she didn't belong in War.

When Tevin first saw her, he decided he wanted her. After all that happened, though, he was determined to keep her safe.

Cassandra fit against his body perfectly, molding to him as though she belonged there.

Too bad she didn't belong in the pack.

Wait? Where had that thought come from? What was he thinking? Of course, she didn't belong in his pack.

Whatever happened was a one night only kind of thing.

They moved further into the corner of the bar, away from any prying eyes, especially the prying eyes of that man who intervened with those males. It shouldn't have bothered Tevin that she knew him. It wasn't any of his business, but he didn't like that she paid attention to another male while pressed against his body.

"Who was that man?"

"Which man? There are lots of men here."

"The one you yelled at, said it was all his fault."

"Ah, no one. Just someone who suggested I come here." She answered, but it didn't answer his question.

He slid behind the table and pulled her along with him. "That beer good? Or do you want another?"

"It's fine."

As though proving a point, she lifted the bottle to her lips and sipped. He watched its voyage for all of three seconds and wanted to rip the bottle from her hands. Tevin didn't want anyone or thing touching her lips.

Fuck. He wished he could take her some place better, but nothing better was still open.

She placed the bottle down and gave him all her attention.

Shit, her eyes were more blue than when he first saw them. He would have been happy spending the rest of the night looking into her eyes. Hell, not even the night, the rest of his life.

Wait.

What?

Tevin shook his head, getting his thoughts back into place.

"So why did you come to the Dirty Whistle?"

"It was suggested." She scanned the room, looking at everyone still inside the bar.

"Yeah, you said that, but come to a bar alone? You don't look like you belong in War."

"Neither do you."

Shit, she had a tongue on her. For a moment Tevin wondered what else she could do with her tongue.

"So, why me?"

"Why not you?" Tevin reached for her hand and tugged her closer.

"Really? You're going with that line? Of everything, you could have said, you're going with why not?" His answer hadn't impressed her one bit.

"I already said. You don't look like you belong here. If things keep going the way they are, you could get hurt. And I'm not going to let that happen." Shit. His mouth was running away from him. Tevin drank his beer before he said anything more.

"Who says you won't hurt me?"

"Cassie, baby, I couldn't ever hurt you." He set the beer down and reached for her hand, squeezing it. "I swear, I will never cause you harm."

Cassandra rolled her eyes and gave him a halfhearted smile. It didn't matter if she thought he was delivering another line to her. Tevin wouldn't break his word. He never had, and he wouldn't start now.

Tevin dropped her hand and wrapped his arm back around her waist. His fingers skimmed down her hip before circling back up to her waist. She sipped her beer and didn't pull away from his touch. Instead, she leaned into him. Sending a silent message to keep going.

A message he didn't plan on ignoring.

He didn't want to frighten her with the question of your place or mine. Although he didn't have a place. At least not one he could bring her to.

Cassandra didn't look like the type of girl who'd get it on in the middle of a bar. Plus, she was wearing jeans. Jeans didn't make things easy for a quickie in a dark corner of a bar.

Although...

Nope. Not going there. Cassandra was classy and not classy with a k. She didn't deserve anonymous sex in the middle of a crowded bar. He'd figure something else out. Even if it took all night.

Cassandra sipped her beer, and he stared at her lips. The way her mouth wrapped around the bottle sent his imagination into a tailspin of pornographic images. By the way his cock hardened, it agreed.

She put her bottle down and cocked her head to the side. Okay, forget her mouth. He wanted to nibble and suck at the pale skin of her neck. And then kiss his way to her lips.

"What are your plans, Tev?"

The sound of his name coming from her husky voice almost buckled his knees.

"Who said I had any?"

"Well, you came across a bar to stand by me, then invited me to join you here. So what was your plan?"

Tevin didn't answer her. Instead, he bent his head slightly and pressed his lips to her temping mouth.

No immediate slap, and she didn't pull away. A definite win in Tevin's book. He brushed the tip of his tongue along the swell of her bottom lip, tasting the beer she'd been drinking. As soon as her lips parted, his tongue darted in, and he turned them around so his back was to the bar, shielding her from any onlookers. Not that anyone could see them or might want to see them, but Tevin liked the idea that none of the other men would be able to look at her. The move drove his wolf crazy. Not being able to see the room was dangerous, but Tevin was beyond the point of caring.

Keeping a hand on her hip, he wrapped his arm around her shoulder and pulled her closer. Cassandra leaned in, and his hand slipped to the back of her head. He controlled the kiss and her movements. And she didn't resist.

Finally, he pulled away and breathed in deeply, filling his lungs with her intoxicating scent. "Cassie."

She opened her eyes and gazed up at him. The tip of her tongue flicked the corner of her mouth, and he growled at the sight. When he bent down to kiss her again, he slipped his fingers behind the waistband of her jeans and brushed the back of his fingers along her soft skin.

At his touch, her arousal flared, and he growled again. He needed more of her. She wanted to know his plans so badly. Well, then, he'd have to show her. Before he returned to Broken Peak, he was going to get inside her, touch heaven, then walk away before he brought any danger to her life.

Her hips pressed against his, encouraging him.

He wrapped her hair around his fingers and pulled her head back, separating them, so he could kiss her jawline. When he reached her ear, he bit down on her earlobe and tugged. She moaned, a soft purring sound, and his cock jumped to attention.

Tevin needed to know Cassandra wanted this as badly as he did. He wouldn't take anything from her she wasn't willing to give.

"Cassie, do you want this?" He whispered. His fingers moved closer to the button of her jeans, giving her a taste of where they would go as long as she agreed.

She nodded. But it wasn't enough. He needed to hear the word. Tevin kept his fingers wrapped in her head, stopping the movement.

"Use your words, Cassie. Do you want this?" He stretched his finger down inside her jeans until the tip brushed against the elastic band of her panties.

She moaned out a soft yes. Loud enough for Tevin to hear.

Tevin pounced. His mouth found hers and his fingers popped the button of her jeans. As soon as his hand slipped beneath her panties, Cassandra wrapped her arms around his neck. He slid two fingers into her as his tongue slipped into her mouth. His thumb pressed against her clit as his fingers stroked into her.

Their kiss deepened, muffling her soft moans. The sounds she made were for him and no one else.

Her breasts rubbed against his chest and for a moment, he wished they were alone, so he could see them. As much as he wanted to kiss them and admire her bare body, feeling them would have to be enough.

They were already playing a dangerous game. Calling Bray to come and bail Tevin out of jail was the last thing the pack needed. He was fairly sure a lot more had happened at the dirty whistle, but probably in one of the grungy bathrooms. And no way in hell would he take her into the dirty as shit bathroom.

That thought was almost enough to yank him back into reality. It wasn't like a darkened corner of the bar was better than the bathroom. But then her hand pressed against his cock, and she squeezed. All the second-thoughts he was having fled.

His fingers continued moving inside with his thumb on her clit and pulled away from her mouth. A pink blush graced her cheeks. He wasn't sure if it was because of his fingers or the chance of getting caught, but he didn't care as long as he played some role in causing her to flush.

Tevin slid a third finger into her. "Do you want more?"

"Yes." She hissed. Her hips bucked against his hand, and she leaned back against the wall.

The logistics of lowering her jeans just enough and freeing his cock from the confines of his jeans took several minutes to figure out. But they persevered and managed it all without having to resort to the grungy bathroom.

When her fingers wrapped around his bare cock, it took all his self-control not to throw her on the table and take her.

He pulled his fingers from her, but stared into her blue eyes as he slid his fingers into his mouth. This would be his only chance to taste her, and he didn't plan on losing it. As he cleaned her from his fingers, he studied her response.

Cassandra licked her lips, wetting them, and Tevin groaned.

He needed more from her, but their location made it impossible. Instead, he'd have to be content with what they could have.

He reached down and lifted her leg, wrapping it around his hip. "Cassie, baby, you ready?"

"Yes."

That one word was all it took.

With the poor lighting in the bar and where they stood in the corner, he wasn't worried about being caught. If anyone glanced at them, they'd look like a couple making out.

His hand cradled her ass, supporting her as he lifted her enough for the head of his cock to press against the tight entrance of her pussy.

Fuck, she was tight.

He bent his knees slightly, and it was enough for him to slide into her.

"So wet and tight, Cassie." Tevin growled into her ear.

As he slid his cock deeper into, he covered her mouth with his. His other arm wrapped around her waist, and he drew her closer while her body grew accustomed to his size.

He wished he could touch her bare skin, to feel her body against his. Instead, he'd have to imagine it. His palm pressed her head closer, and he deepened the kiss to match the slow movements of his cock inside her. The possessive kiss claimed her as his. He would make her his for the night, and then he'd walk away. Keeping her away from the danger of his world.

She moaned into his kiss and he swallowed the noises. As much as he wished he could hear her screaming out in pleasure, the sounds would have to remain in his imagination.

Cassandra's arms tightened around his neck and ground her hips against his. The small movement pushed Tevin close to the edge. He wanted to make the moment last. If he only had one night with her, even if he wanted more, then he was going to make it last for as long as possible.

She writhed against him. Tevin wished he could reach between them to press against her clit and help her along, but his hands were otherwise occupied with supporting her. Eventually, the sensations were too much for Tevin to handle. Pressing her against the wall, he slid his hand that was behind her head, down her body to her hip. Stuck between his body and the wall, Tevin held her in place and thrust hard into her.

The scent of her arousal blossomed into the air and Tevin lost hold of what little control he had left.

He thrust harder, and she matched his intensity with her kiss.

She was as close as he was. Her body tensed and tightened around his cock. He pushed his cock in deeper, and her pussy tightening around him grew stronger.

Past the point of holding back. Not that he wanted to. He grabbed hold of her hips and pulled her tight against him as he came hard. Their mouths, locked together in a fierce kiss, silenced the loud moans coming from both of them.

Staying inside her, he tightened his embrace. Even though he knew better, he wasn't ready to let go of her. At least not yet. He kissed the line of her jaw to her ear, then back to her lips. Except this kiss didn't have any of the hunger from before. The need remained, but his lips were gentle. He took his time, nuzzling the skin he could touch as the small waves of pleasure rolled through her body.

She loosened her arms from his neck and pressed her forehead against his shoulder. While their racing hearts slowed, they stayed joined together in silence. He combed his fingers through her hair and pressed his lips to the top of her head and breathed in her scent, committing it to memory. This was the only time he'd have her in his arms, and he didn't want to forget it.

No last names, no strings, and no promises.

CHAPTER SEVEN

CASSANDRA sat on the toilet of the small inn and stared at the white stick in her hand. Like she could magic away the second pink line. Or all the second pink lines from the seven pregnancy tests she'd already taken. The little plastic sticks lined up neatly on the counter, mocking her.

Five weeks passed, and she was still in War. Every time she packed and attempted to check out, that urge to stay returned. The worst part about it was that even though she knew the source of that compulsion, she couldn't break it. She'd tried. And to add insult to injury, she couldn't find that man with the old magic. He was still around, that much she could tell, but she couldn't find him.

Memaw wasn't any help. In fact, her grandma had been dodging her calls like a pro.

And now, to add to it all, she was pregnant.

"Okay, Moose. I guess I have to go back to the Dirty Whistle every night, find the guy, and hand him a stick.

The dog cocked his head to the side, listening to her words even if he didn't understand them.

"And then what?" She closed her eyes, briefly wondering if maybe she could pretend the two pink lines weren't there. Of all the available options, crying seemed best. But she'd already spent most of the day crying and nothing more to show for it than eight positive pregnancy tests.

The eighth stick joined the others and Cassandra pressed her hands against her face.

"What am I going to do, Moose?" She spread her fingers and peeked out at the dog. "Do I tell Memaw? Or do I find a way to quietly take care of it?"

She hated that phrase. *Take care of it.* There was no taking care of something like cleaning up a spilled drink. With a quick sweep of her hand, she brushed away the tears. "I don't know his last name or where he lives."

Her head fell back, and she screamed at the ceiling.

Just over a minute later, a sharp knock came from the door. Moose jumped to his feet and barked. He had to let everyone know he knew someone was outside, and he wasn't at all happy about it.

"Coming." Cassandra stood and left the bathroom, closing the door behind her and blocking the sight of the army of pregnancy tests.

"Is everything okay in there?" A deep voice asked from the other side of the door.

"Yeah. Hold on a sec. Moose, go lie down and stop barking all ready." She pointed to the bed Moose used when he wasn't sleeping in the bed next to her. He didn't obey, but at least he stopped barking.

"Sorry, had a moment there. I'll keep it down." Cassandra opened the door and peeked her head out into the hallway. The man from the bar, the one with old magic, not the shifter she was looking for, stood in the hallway.

Her eyes narrowed, and she idly wondered how her magic would fare against his.

"Are you sure everything's alright, Ms Voisin?"

"It's fine. Just a moment of temporary frustration."

"If you're sure then." The man stepped back from the door and turned toward the stairway. Before he disappeared, he looked over his shoulder at her. "If you decide it's not temporary, ask the manager to contact me."

"I don't know your name." Although he was a near stranger to her, the man was also the closest thing she had to a friend in War. Assuming someone with magic as old as his had any friends.

"I'm Alex. I own this inn."

Her eyes popped open. Old magic living in War and not visiting? That knowledge was a surprise. Not as big as the surprise currently incubating in her uterus, but still unexpected.

"Have a good evening, Ms Voisin." Alex said as he descended the staircase.

"Well shit." Cassandra closed the door and re locked it.

She threw herself down on the bed and covered her face. How had she been so stupid? Logic and all the common sense her grandmother taught her must have gone on sabbatical and left her libido in charge. This wasn't supposed to happen.

Nowhere in any of the books, assuming she believed in those stupid prophecies, said anything about her getting pregnant. Except the string of pregnancy tests proved that sentiment incorrect.

She sat up in bed and stared at Moose, who was still sitting in front of the door, staring at it. It would have been nice if her dog could have helped her out, but she didn't think he could. She needed to find the shifter first. Then she could inform him he was going to be a father. Without knowing anything more about him, she'd start at the Dirty Whistle. Maybe, if she was lucky, she'd find someone who knew where he lived or, you know, his last name. Sadly, the bar probably didn't allow dogs.

Moose came over to her and pressed his head down on the bed. "I know, buddy, I wish you could come too. Promise me you won't do your crying thing when I'm gone. I think my scream wore out my good-will with the other guests."

Moose's tail thumped against the floor.

"Thanks for understanding."

Now, if only she could turn Moose into a stylist. What was she supposed to wear to hang out at a dive bar while waiting for her baby daddy to show up, so she could inform him he's the said baby daddy?

Jeans and a sweater. No muss and no fuss. Although, since it was now February, War wasn't as cold as it had been when she first arrived over a month ago.

Holy crap, had she been here for that long?

Cassandra stripped out of her sweats, tugged on a pair of jeans, and pulled on a cotton turtleneck sweater with a thick cable pattern. Her hair got the ponytail treatment, but her face didn't receive any of the cosmetics hanging out next to the lineup of positive pregnancy tests.

One last check in the mirror to make sure she didn't look like she was trying to not look like she was trying.

Well crap.

The button of her jeans tugged at the buttonhole. Surely it was because of the two packages of Oreos she ate and not because of the whole positive pregnancy test thing. Maybe she should change into a longer sweater. Nope, nope, nope. Then she *would* be trying not to try.

Before she chickened out, Cassandra refilled Moose's water, gave him his dinner, and slipped out of the room. The bar was only a few blocks away, so she walked, which would give her a few extra minutes to come up with the best thing to say if she managed to be lucky enough to find Tevin at the bar.

There was the lighthearted approach. "Hey, not sure if you remember me, but around five weeks ago, we met, had amazing sex in the corner of a bar, and guess what? You're gonna be a daddy."

Or the more serious approach. "Hi, I'm Cassandra. We spent an evening together about five weeks ago. Anyway, I'm pregnant and I haven't decided anything yet, but don't worry, I don't expect you to be responsible."

None of those sentences seemed like a good place to start the "surprise, I'm pregnant" conversation.

Along the route to the bar, she discovered a small stationery shop that sold cards. Maybe she could find one with a store on it, then she only had to write the words "Guess what?" on the inside.

Wait, when did War get a card store? Cassandra stopped in the middle of the sidewalk and looked around the neighborhood. All the buildings had a fresh coat of paint and the windows were clean. The street was clean. And the biggest surprise was the Dirty Whistle. It still had the same name, but the last adjective she'd use to describe the establishment was dirty. The tables even had chairs.

Great, if it was no longer a dive Tevin might have found a new place to frequent.

From what she could see through the window, the customers were the same, though.

Well, now or never. Cassandra walked up to the door, stretched her hand out to the handle, then promptly turned around and walked to the building next door. She completed that routine three times before actually opening the door and stepping into the bar.

A woman stood behind the bar and offered Cassandra a wide smile. One that almost sent Cassandra running in the opposite direction. Shifter magic rolled across the entire bar. It wasn't from the patrons either. The bartender was a shifter.

Well, that was good news, right? If a shifter was tending bar, then she totally had to know Tevin.

Cassandra returned the smile a few seconds too late, then stepped to the bar. She found an empty stool and sat down. Everything was clean, even the area right under the counter was clean.

"What can I get for you?" The bartender stood in front of her and slapped a coaster down on the bar.

"Um, do you have any juice?" She probably shouldn't be drinking, and only ordering water wouldn't make the bartender happy.

"Orange juice okay?"

"Sure. And how about a bag of those chips." Cassandra pointed to the chip display next to the large cash register.

"That's it?"

"Yeah. Having a bit of a salt craving."

A few minutes later, the bartender returned with her order. "Anything else?"

"Yeah, I'm looking for someone. His name is Tevin?"

"No one named Tevin works here."

"He'd be a customer. I met him here a month ago."

"Nope, sorry." The bartender turned and hurried to a customer on the other end of the bar.

Cassandra stared at her back. The shifter definitely knew Tevin. She just wasn't willing to help Cassandra. And it wasn't like she could force the shifter to tell her where Tevin was, or admit she knew Tevin.

The plan she came up with in the inn was not a well-planned out one. She grabbed a pen from her purse and the coaster in front of her.

With a quick scribble, she added her name, number, and the hotel room she was staying in. When she finished, she waved for the bartender, who took her time coming back, but eventually came to a stop in front of Cassandra.

"If you happen to run into someone named Tevin, could you give this to him please?"

The bartender looked down at the coaster, then back up at Cassandra, but didn't reach for the coaster.

"Please, just in case?" The plaintive whine in her voice made her cringe. Why was she begging a complete stranger to take the coaster with her information?

The bartender looked right at Cassandra and blinked before walking away. Without the coaster.

Well, crap. She sat there alone in a bar, with a glass of orange juice and a bag of chips. In her fantasy, the scene had played out differently. Like Tevin was at the Dirty Whistle, sitting alone because she couldn't imagine having a conversation with anyone nearby.

While she sipped the orange juice, no point in letting it go to waste, she wondered what her future would be like with her unborn child.

The glass dropped back to the counter with a quiet slam. For the first time since suspecting then learning she was pregnant, Cassandra used the words unborn and child together. She wasn't sure where the decision came from, but at some point between peeing on the pregnancy tests and walking through town, she came to a conclusion.

The more she thought about it, the more she was okay with her conclusion. It didn't matter if she found Tevin or what he thought about it. She was going to keep her baby.

Well, crap, she was channeling Madonna, now.

Leaving a ten on the counter for her drink and chips along with the coaster, just in case the bartender changed her mind, she slipped off the stool. As she left the bar, she ran through her next set of options now that she had decided she was having the child.

Her grandma could help raise the baby. But what about the shifter side of things? As far as Cassandra knew, shifters and witches hadn't ever had children. It wasn't that they didn't get along as much as history had a long memory and kept them from mixing. She'd be surprised if most shifters knew about witches.

The supernatural world was a disconnected mess at the best of times. And if the writings were accurate, at war with each other instead of being allies.

She wasn't sure about the biology of mixing supernaturals. And if she had a child who could shift, well, then she'd have to find a nice group of shifters who would be willing to help her.

The walk back to the inn took far less time than the walk to the bar, and before she knew it, she was in front of the door to her room. When she opened the door, Moose greeted her with some barking, lots of jumping, and a tail moving a mile a minute.

"Hey buddy. Guess what? You're going to have a baby to contend with in eight months. Or is it nine because of the weeks thing?" Cassandra spoke to her dog while petting his head. "I can never remember."

Settling onto the bed with Moose curled up next to her, she imagined what it would be like having a half witch, half shifter baby.

CHAPTER EIGHT

"DANIELLE finally cracked through the burner phone we found in the room the Black Hills Pack were staying in. Turns out another pack is in play. One from the southeast." Vixen sat across from Tevin in Bray's office. She liked to handle pack concerns in the quiet room, away from the big ears of a child who liked to repeat everything he heard. "She's also been getting pings on her system. Two numbers are coming up over and over. They might not be connected, but both numbers can be traced to War."

Tevin had no clue why she was talking with him. Vixen didn't usually share specific information until it was time to act.

This didn't sound like a government thing. They had slowed their attempts to infiltrate pack territory in the past few months. Proba-bly because Vixen disappeared for a few days every so often, never telling anyone where she went, and had "conversations" with the people making decisions. Plus, she handled the government stuff herself.

However, with Delia's arrival, they had another set of problems to deal with. Other shifters. Vixen and Bray kept things simple. They only responded when loners or packs crossed them. The Black Hills Pack had been one of those problems, but Tevin thought Vixen had handled it.

Unless another pack got it into their minds that they could still grab Delia and gain more power.

"You and Finley are going to check on what's happening. Start with this number." She slid a piece of paper with a phone number and last known location. "We think it has ties to that pack in the southwest. Take care of it."

"Um, take care of it?" Tevin asked. He wasn't sure what she meant and didn't want to fuck things up.

"Find out any information you can, then eliminate them if they're a threat."

Fuck him sideways. Vixen and Bray had a new strategy.

"Should we bring them back here?"

"Nope."

"Won't that leave a mess in town?"

"We have someone who can help us clean up, but we want the message sent to everyone and not just the problem packs."

"Um, okay, but why me and Finley? Isn't Leighton better at these things."

Vixen cocked her head to the side and peered at him with her in that weird raptor like way of hers. "Because you won't find it distasteful. Leighton will feel guilty, Jackson will argue, and Allard won't understand it."

Yeah, she knew him better than he liked. After being kicked from his pack while still a pup, he didn't much care for the way most were run. Broken Peak was different, but that was because of Bray and Vixen.

"But Finley?"

"Maggie's past with her Gaze gives him a different perspective from the others. More similar to yours."

Tevin leaned back in the chair. Okay, this was weird. Vixen wasn't bugging him about questioning things. And why was she basically putting him in charge of things. None of this made sense.

"You do a good job making others think you aren't capable or responsible. But if something happens to me or Bray, you're the one most capable of making the decisions that will need to be made."

"You realize that doesn't help with the whole you being able to read our minds theory."

"Relax. Your expression revealed everything, something we'll have to work on. But it didn't take a mind reader to figure it out."

Tevin looked down at the slip of paper. "A dive hotel? That's odd."

"We're not sure about this southeast pack. It might be someone they hired, or someone from their own pack."

"They have money?"

That was the thing with smaller packs, they usually had money, but no power and didn't understand why not.

"Looks like it, from the accounts Danielle pulled up."

"So it's probably not someone from their own pack."

"Maybe, maybe not. It could be a ploy, a vacant room, or it might be they don't want to risk getting caught at The Old Jail."

"Okay, so that leaves the kind of message you want us to leave."

"A loud one." Vixen said, as she nodded toward the door. "Make sure you gear up before going. Protective clothing too."

Well, okay then. The conversation was over, and Tevin was dismissed. He stood and left the office. "Alright, Vixen."

First, he needed to find Finley. He expected to have to look all over, but he was waiting out in the hallway.

"Bray sent me."

"Vixen has something we need to take care of. Let's go."

Tevin strode down the hallway to the door at the end. The room behind it housed all their weapons and gear. And access to the garage. No one would see them leave, which was a good thing. No one would ask them questions.

"Where to?" Finley asked.

"War." Tevin handed Finley the paper with the address. "You driving?"

"Sure. Hey, Maddie called. Some girl stopped by the bar looking for you."

A small group of mountain lion shifters under Gareth lived close to Broken Peak. Maddie was Gareth's niece and at some point convinced her uncle to buy the Dirty Whistle.

"What do you mean some girl? And why didn't she call me?"

"Guess she couldn't reach you. And don't know. She just said that some girl was asking about you."

What girl would stop by the Dirty Whistle? There was only one woman Tevin could think of and one he'd been spending the past four weeks trying to forget. Not that he excelled at that particular task. Tevin had been spending more than a few nights at the Dirty Whistle, but he spent them alone.

Shit. Change of plans. They needed to stop by the Dirty Whistle first.

They finished gearing up and headed out the back door to the garage.

"We need to make a quick detour."

Finley gaped at him with wide eyes, but didn't say anything. Tevin ignored him.

They drove to town not talking. Which was for the best.

It wasn't like the pack hadn't known about the visits to the Dirty Whistle. Or that he ignored every woman in the bar and sat alone drinking his beer. He told himself he wasn't hanging out hoping she might make an appearance.

And what if it wasn't even her asking about him. He wanted it to be, but at the same time he hoped it wasn't. If they had to deal with packs intent on going after the Broken Peak Pack and not in a polite way, he didn't want her seeing that. That night was the best night in Tevin's life, but he didn't deserve her, and she sure as fuck didn't deserve him or the life she'd have at Broken Peak.

Finley pulled the SUV in front of the Dirty Whistle. "We going in or should we have Maddie come out?"

Tevin peered through the windshield and into the bar. It didn't look busy. Probably because it was a Sunday night. Maddie and one of her cousins stood behind the counter not doing much but cleaning the counter.

"Call her, I guess."

Finley picked up the phone and dialed. From inside the bar, Maddie reached into her pocket and pulled out her cell phone.

It was easier to not think about Cassandra when no one mentioned her. But now that the hint of her had been brought up, he couldn't get her out of his mind. He remembered her scent, the way her body fit against his, the way he felt inside her. He remembered every fucking detail, even if he didn't want to.

Maddie came out from the bar, opened the back door of the SUV, and slid into the backseat.

"You have a fan, Tev. I didn't tell her anything, but she didn't deserve the cold shoulder."

Tevin didn't turn around to look at Maddie. "She deserves Broken Peak problems even less."

"When she walked out, she was crying."

His head snapped around. "What did you do to her?"

"Nothing. Just what you said. Tell her we don't know you. And I don't think she realized she was crying. But the girl was hurt." Maddie glared at Tevin. "You come into the bar almost every night, turn away every woman who looks twice at you, but you want us to run her off when we do finally see her."

"Whatever." Tevin returned to staring out the windshield. "We have a concern, want to join us?"

"Sure, why not. It's a slow night." Maddie grinned. "Let me run in and tell Bella."

As soon as Maddie left the car, Finley spoke up.

"Really? You're bringing Maddie along?"

"She's more than capable of handling herself."

"Yeah, but Gareth will kill you if she gets so much as a scrape."

"They're our allies, right?" Vixen's words about making the tough decisions came back to him. "It's time we start working together more. Especially now that you all are mated."

"Hey, we still pull our weight." Finley protested.

"Not saying you don't. But I've been on as many patrols with Maddie and her cousins as I have with my own packmates. And she'll be good to have along."

What he didn't say was that when it came time to leave the message, Tevin was worried Finley might not be able to handle it. Not only would Maddie be able to handle it, but her skills would make her a bigger asset than Finley. Before Finley could offer another protest, Maddie climbed back into the car.

"So, what's this concern?" Maddie asked as she pulled her seat belt into place.

"Some traffic Danielle discovered. We're pretty sure it's coming from that pack in the southeast."

"The one that hired those three wolves who went after Delia?"

"Yes and no," Tevin answered. "From the burner phone we found, it looks like they only hired one of the wolves. The other two thought the job was a snatch and grab."

"Wait, I thought that the Northwest Pack was responsible. Or Spencer whatever his last name was."

"Spencer Pearce's arrangement with the three wolves from Black Hills was a last-minute thing, and they had two different goals." Tevin explained how the two of the three wolves from the Black Hills Pack only intended on kidnapping Delia. The third wolf had orders, not from his Alpha, to kill her. And Spencer's plan included killing Allard. "From the looks of it, a Black Hills wolf took a few extra jobs that were off the books. And the pack from the southeast hasn't given up on their plans."

Maddie shook her head slowly from side to side. "Well shit, you guys have a lot more drama going on than we all realized."

Finley grinned at her in the rear-view mirror. "You have no idea."

"At least it's not boring." Maddie returned his grin. "I put the coaster in the back office, you know."

Tevin wasn't going to tell Finley to turn around so Maddie could run back in and get it. He'd have a phone number, hell, he might have an address. Maybe, if he could play everything right, he'd be able to keep her separate from the dangers of Broken Peak. Except he knew better. The other males spent most of their time worrying about the safety of their mates, and in Jackson's case, also his son.

As much as he wanted the coaster, the best course of action would be to have Maddie toss it. To get rid of it, shred it up, hell, she should burn the fucking thing. But everyone knew he wouldn't say those words. Instead, he opted for an acknowledgment that was totally a coward's answer. "Fine."

The drive to the motel didn't take much time.

The target had the decency to actually be inside a hotel room that was at the end of the building. No chance of disturbing anyone else. It also made it easier to take care of business, which Maddie helped with, more than Finley.

The shifter had been hired by the pack and wasn't a member. A hired gun. He had also been nice enough to give them the last name and address of another contact. He didn't have the details of how they were related, only that he had been warned someone else had brought them in to interfere with the Broken Peak Pack.

They were about to pay Mr. Voisin, currently staying at The Old Jail Inn, a visit. Too bad he was staying at the inn. They'd have to keep things quiet or take Voisin back to pack territory. Neither option was good.

Maddie stepped out of the motel room and next to Tevin. She'd cleaned up the scene enough to make it look like a suicide to everyone who wasn't a shifter.

"We good?" He asked her.

Maddie said nothing, not even a gesture. But then she didn't need to and Tevin didn't need to ask the question. Of course, they were good. Maddie was efficient at cleaning up things. And Tevin learned he was more than efficient at extracting information.

What was more, he might have actually enjoyed it a little. He figured the enjoyment came from getting all his frustrations out. Beat the shit out of someone and suddenly not seeing Cassandra for over a month wasn't that horrible. The not seeing her was still crappy, but not as crappy.

"So, off to Voisin's then?" Finley joined their small huddle outside the room.

"Yeah. Might as well clean up everything before heading back." Plus if they took care of Voisin now, Tevin could have Finley drop him off at the Dirty Whistle. And then he could spend the rest of the night drinking alone.

Tevin walked away from the motel room to the SUV and the others followed. Just because the motel was a dive, and the room was far away from any of the others with guests, didn't mean they needed to be obvious and stand out for everyone to see.

As they got into the car, Maddie and Tevin scanned the area. No one was out or walking down the street. If their luck held out, no one would suspect the death was anything more than a suicide.

Finley started the car and headed to the inn. "What's the plan?"

"I guess we grab Voisin and take him out to the woods." The more Tevin thought about it, he realized it would be impossible to keep things quiet at the inn. Plus one of Vixen's "friends" had ties to the inn, and he didn't want to burn that bridge.

He watched the town pass by the window and wondered if maybe, the one night he wasn't at the Dirty Whistle, Cassandra would make another appearance. She showed up at the bar earlier. Maybe she'd come back hoping to catch him?

Tevin wasn't sure if not being at the Dirty Whistle tonight was a good thing or a bad thing.

"Where should I park?" Finley asked.

"The employees have a door in the alley they use." Maddie answered.

"Maddie and I will go in the front, then open the back door. Finley, keep the car running, but stay by the door."

Tevin needed to get his head back in the game. They couldn't make a mistake now, not when they were so close to cleaning up everything. Thoughts about Cassandra would only distract him and cause a screw up.

Finley circled the block and found the alley before swinging back around to the front of the building where he dropped Maddie and Tevin off.

As they walked inside the small inn, the young woman behind the front desk smiled and waved at them.

"We're here to visit a friend."

"Oh, okay, do you know their room?"

Maddie returned the smile and the wave back. "Yep, just got off the phone with them. They weren't ready yet and said to come on up."

"All right, have a good night." The woman returned to whatever task she had been working on when they interrupted her.

As they headed up the stairs towards Voisin's room, Tevin should have been worried that it all had seemed too easy. In his experience, nothing was ever simple enough for all the pieces to fall perfectly into place.

CHAPTER NINE

THE tapping on the door followed by Moose barking woke Cassandra up. The clock on the side table said it was only 8:00 pm. She must have fallen asleep while bingeing the latest crime documentary on Netflix. The documentaries were her guilty pleasure, and she couldn't remember the last time she ever fell asleep while watching one.

Something else she could blame on Tevin if she ever got up the nerve to visit the Dirty Whistle again. She was sure she'd find him there later at night. Unless the bartender gave him the head's up that she was on her way in so he could sneak out the back. Maybe that was his thing. Sneaking out the back when all the discarded women came looking for him.

Another knock on the door and more barking from Moose brought her completely out of her semi-sleep state and she stumbled to the door. "Moose, go lie down."

As usual Moose ignored her command, but at least he stopped barking. That man with the old magic was probably back. Alexander had looked too concerned to give up on trying to get her to talk.

She opened the door, prepared to inform him he needed to mind his own business, but the words never left her mouth. In fact, she didn't get her mouth open.

Standing outside her door was the man who caused her emotional roller coaster of a day. And behind him was his partner in crime. The woman who claimed she didn't know anyone named Tevin.

What a little liar.

She tilted her head to the side and looked at the two. They appeared to be as surprised by her opening the door as she was by their standing there. But it wasn't possible. She had to be dreaming. Maybe she wasn't fully awake.

Pulling the door completely open, she stepped back. "Come on in."

Shit, she picked the worst time for opting for comfort. She wasn't even in a pair of yoga pants or something sort of sexy. Nope, fleece pants and an oversized sweatshirt was her wardrobe of choice. It was one step away from being a snuggie.

She never should have left her information on that coaster.

Instead of jumping around like a hyperactive monster, Moose apparently found his will to obey and lied down on his bed.

Tevin stepped into the hotel room, then another until he stood in front of her. He placed his hands on her shoulders and sighed out her name. "Cassie."

Crap. She wanted to be angry. She wanted to yell at him and slap him for having that bartender say she didn't know him. Except she didn't do anything like that. Nope. She stepped closer to Tevin and wrapped her arms around him. Her forehead pressed down on his shoulder and she breathed in.

A second later and he returned her embrace.

With a deep breath she stepped away from him. She didn't want to, but she had a lot of say to him and couldn't say it while he was holding her.

She also couldn't say anything with an audience.

Tevin pressed his palms to her cheeks and looked into her eyes.

"Pack your bags, Cassie."

As much as she hated the thought of losing his touch, she stepped away from him. God, she hadn't realized how much she missed his touch, or wanted it back, but the first thing to say to a girl you hadn't seen in over a month, was not pack a bag. "What? Why should I?"

Tevin closed the distance between them. And this time when his hands held her cheeks, she couldn't pull away from him.

"Pack your bags." He spoke slowly, pausing between each word.

"No." She tried to jerk away, but Tevin didn't allow it. Not that he hurt her, but he was stronger.

"Either you pack your bags or Maddie will. The choice is yours."

She narrowed her eyes at the male shifter in front of her and prepared a spell that would push Tevin and Maddie out of the room. Except the magic didn't listen. The spell fizzled, and all she got for it was the equivalent of an electric shock.

Okay then, she'd have to use words instead. "I haven't seen you in over a month, I don't know where you live or your last name. And Maddie there said she didn't know you. So the answer to packing a bag is no.

Tevin glanced over at Maddie and the shifter slipped into the bathroom. Cassandra used the moment to pull away from him. She wasn't sure where she was going to go and since Moose was still lying down on the bed with all four legs up in the air, he wasn't going to be any help.

Tevin's arms reached around her middle, and he pulled her back until she pressed against his chest.

She froze like a deer caught in the headlights. She didn't think Tevin would hurt her, but having someone touch her stomach set off all the alarms. Except none of them had anything to do with self-preservation and saving herself. It was all about the little entity growing inside her.

At that moment, Cassandra made a decision. Tevin didn't deserve to know he was going to be a father. She'd tell him eventually, but well after they had discussed appropriate boundaries and behavior. Including not showing up at her hotel room and demanding she pack a bag.

"Cassie." The deep growl in his voice rumbled through his chest and down her back.

Her body betrayed her and enjoyed the sensation. She really shouldn't have enjoyed it at all. He lifted her up and carried her to the bed. Instead of setting her down, he sat down and held her in his lap. She tried to squirm away from him, but his arms had too many muscles and his grasp was too strong.

Her appreciation of muscles slipped down the list of things she shouldn't like but secretly did.

"Maddie is going to pack your things. Then you are coming with us. And you aren't going to fight it, Cassie."

Yeah, like that was going to happen. Except the first part was already happening because Maddie came out of the bathroom with Cassie's bag of toiletries and headed right to the drawers and her empty duffel bag. But that didn't mean the second and third things had to happen.

Cassandra went limp in his arms. All dead weight. Just like Moose when she tried to give him a bath. His arms slid up until they circled her ribs instead of her waist. And then she went with the flailing limbs approach. Swinging her arms around, so they hit whatever part of them they could reach and banging her heels into his shins. "Nope. It's not going to happen."

All her efforts resulted in Tevin slipping his hold to her wrists and crossing her arms over her chest. Then he used his leg to keep hers from swinging.

"Stop it, Cassie."

"And who are you to make demands."

"We can talk about it later."

"Now or I scream." As soon as she opened her mouth, his hand covered it.

And Moose still hadn't budged. The little traitor.

Why had all the TV shows made it look easy to get away from someone. She should be clear and running away by now. Instead, she was arguably worse off than when she had started.

Cassandra grumbled behind his hand.

"Cassie, this doesn't have to be so difficult."

When all else fails, go with the toddler approach. She licked his hand. And not in a sexy way either. She'd gross him out if he wasn't letting her go.

His breath skimmed across the side of her neck immediately followed by a gentle bite on the space between her shoulder and neck.

Logic and reason said she shouldn't enjoy it. But her body was not listening to logic and reason. She leaned back against him.

"So help me, Cassie, I will put you over my knee and spank you."

Once more her body ignored logic and reason. But then, if the hard length pressing against her ass was anything to go by, Tevin was ignoring logic and reason too.

Crap.

This was so not how she planned on things happening when she opened the door and saw him standing there.

"Will you behave?"

She nodded since his hand was still covering her mouth, and she couldn't say anything.

"You won't scream?"

She nodded again.

When his hand fell away, she stretched her jaw with a large yawn. "Why did you come?"

"It's a long and complicated story." Tevin sighed, and he loosened his arm still holding her arms in front of her chest. The firm grasp turned to a gentle embrace as he cradled her against his chest.

"Hey Tev?" Maddie looked over at them while holding three bags. "I got the dog's things packed too."

Oh, crap. The bathroom. Cassandra completely forgot about the pregnancy tests in the small garbage can. They had been camping out on top of the empty boxes with the words Early Response and Pregnancy in big bold letters.

She had to have seen them. Cassandra stared at Maddie and pulled what little magic she could to compel the female shifter not to say anything.

"Ready?" Maddie asked.

With a deep breath of relief, Cassandra closed her eyes and nodded.

"Give us a few. Let Finley know there's been a change of plans and bring the dog with you."

Change of plans? Cassandra was a change of plans? And there was someone else?

The flight instinct kicked in and she pushed off of Tevin's lap. Or she would have if his arms hadn't tightened around her.

Maddie looked at them for a moment before shrugging her shoulders. With a whistle, she walked out the door and Moose followed right behind her, tail wagging as hard as ever.

She also closed the door behind her. For the first time since, well since ever, Cassandra was alone with Tevin.

"Cassie, I need you to come with us. Trust me on this. Okay?" His thumb rubbed across her wrist, soothing her. "It's better if you walk with me, but I will carry you out of here if I have to. It's up to you."

But the choice wasn't really a choice because she ended up in the same position, regardless. Either way she was going with him, the only choice was how she went with him.

"You're kidnapping me. And you can add dog napping too."

"Fuck, Cassie. Just trust me. I swore I'd never hurt you and I meant it."

His words pushed at all her buttons. She jumped from his lap and spun on her heel. She had every intention of going off on him, no matter what he said.

"What do you call telling Maddie that she doesn't know you if I come asking? That hurt me, Tevin. And now you show up here and demand I pack a bag and go with you? You didn't bother to ask how I was doing or say the word hello." The stream of words left her mouth and nothing would stop them. "Maybe I have a boyfriend now and maybe he'll come through the door. And maybe he's promised me something more than a quick fuck in the corner of a bar."

Crap. Somehow she had a hypothetical boyfriend.

"You have a boyfriend?" Tevin slowly stood and stalked towards her.

His hands tightened into fists and Cassandra realized she was in way over her head. Shifters could get possessive and from the way his muscles tightened beneath his clothing and his eyes flashed a bright silver, Tevin had hit that mark. This wasn't a typical anger that came with raised voices. Tevin was in a rage and his target was her hypothetical boyfriend.

Cassandra could have calmed him down. All it would have taken was a few words. No, she didn't have a boyfriend. But she was still pissed at him, and she wasn't letting him off that easy. Especially not after she walked out of that bar wondering if she'd ever see him again.

His arms circled her waist, and he hoisted her over his shoulder.

"The talking part of the evening is over. We're going. Now."

She kicked her feet against his chest, but his other arm clasped her legs to his body.

"Shoes." Right at the top of the list of the stupidest things ever to say in the middle of a kidnapping. It had been the hypothetical boyfriend comment, but shoes took its place with no contest. "I need shoes."

Tevin grabbed the pair of trendy, but ugly, Uggs from the floor all while muttering the words pain and ass. He slipped them on to her feet, but they sort of hung there. Like she was hanging off his shoulder.

"We're leaving now. You aren't going to make a scene, are you, Cassie? If you scream or raise your voice, I'll spank you until you can't sit down for a week." To emphasize his point, his hand came down hard on her ass.

She reached behind her and rubbed the sting while hoping that Tevin hadn't heard the soft moan that left her mouth. Stupid traitorous body. She'd have to have a long chat with it later on about listening to the logic and reason part of her brain.

Tevin opened the door and though she knew she'd probably get another spanking, she spoke.

"Wait. Moose has a stuffed toy. We can't leave it behind or he'll have a fit."

Another round of pain and ass came from Tevin as he circled back to grab the toy.

As they headed down the hallway to the back set of stairs usually only used by the staff, Cassandra wondered if it was worth banging on one of the doors. The problem with her idea was that she didn't know which rooms had guests. If she knocked on the door to an empty room, it wouldn't have been worth it.

Logic and reason must have joined sides with her body because as soon as the thought came to mind, other thoughts pushed it away. Thoughts about how his hand felt on her ass or how it would feel to have his bare skin touch hers.

It was time to face things. She was going with Tevin and fighting it wasn't going to make it not happen. Besides, her mind had given up on offering any more protests and her body was in full agreement with the "going along with Tevin" plan.

CHAPTER TEN

TEVIN dumped Cassie in the backseat of the SUV, placing her between Maddie and him. Her dog was sitting comfortably in the front seat, keeping Finley company. As soon as Finley lowered the window, Moose stuck his head out the window, as happy as could be. Cassie, on the other hand, was anything but happy. She was pissed.

For the entire drive back to Broken Peak, she glared at him. But he didn't care. He needed to figure this shit out and hopefully come up with something before they got back.

Her world and his should never have crossed, and yet there they were. He had figured that by staying away from her, she'd be safe, but fate or destiny or whatever the fuck it was gave him the middle finger instead.

Now that she was in his world, she was also in his life. No fucking way would he let anyone touch her. She was off limits to everyone. Even Vixen.

When he came to a stoplight, Finley glanced back at them and smiled at Cassie. Both Tevin and his wolf wanted to claw Finley's eyes out for looking at her. But that possessive shit wasn't really aimed at Finley, it was aimed at her fucking boyfriend. If he ever saw the man, he'd rip his throat out.

"Hey, we need to make a quick stop." When the light turned green, Finley drove through the intersection and pulled up along the curb in front of a bakery. "I promised Pocket."

Without any more explanation, he hopped out of the car and dashed into the bakery.

"Pocket?" Cassie asked.

"Later." Tevin growled.

Maddie reached down between her legs and grabbed a bottle of tequila then handed it to Tevin. "I grabbed it from the bar. Figured we might need it."

Tevin opened the bottle. She had been right, he did need a strong drink. After taking a few swallows from the bottle, he held it out to Cassie. "Take a drink."

She eyed the bottle like it was going to bite her and shook her head. Since they showed up at her hotel room, she'd fought him every step of the way. She needed to learn that she had to listen to him if they had any hope of surviving this. And the sooner she learned it, the better.

"Fucking take a drink, Cassie."

Her lips clamped together in a tight line as she shook her head from side to side.

"Sheesh, I drank from it, so it's not poisoned or anything."

"Here." Maddie handed her a bottle of water.

"Thank you." Cassie twisted off the cap and drank some of the water, but she still wouldn't look at him.

Tevin didn't think that things could be any worse, but they seemed to be doing just that. He looked over Cassie's head at Maddie, who gave him a small head shake. Maybe she knew something he didn't, which he definitely didn't like one bit. But he'd give her the benefit of the doubt. This time.

Finley came back to the car with a large cake box and a smaller white bag. As soon as he slid into the driver's seat, he turned around and handed Cassie the bag.

"I wasn't sure what you liked, but the cronuts looked tasty." He then handed Maddie the box. "Keep this safe. Pocket's wanted a cheesecake from this place for a while now."

What? Cronuts? A cheesecake? Had they turned into some kind of food delivery service? Besides, Cassie didn't deserve a treat after the shit she pulled back at the inn. He almost yanked the bag out of her hands, but the way her face lit up as she peered into the bag stopped him. She looked up and gave Finley a wide grin.

What the hell? That grin should have been for Tevin. He should have been the one to give her a treat.

Cassie reached into the bag and pulled out a sugar coated monstrosity, and he couldn't look away from her. Her eyes closed, and she relaxed back against the seat while biting into the gourmet donut. Shit, it was almost pornographic.

He looked up and caught Finley watching her. Tevin didn't think he growled, but Finley quickly turned back around and pulled back on to the road.

When they pulled onto the highway that would take them back home, Tevin wrapped his arm around her shoulders and pulled her closer to him. She didn't protest or pull away and his wolf relaxed.

As soon as she finished the cronut, she licked the sugar from her fingertips, then pulled a second one from the bag. Life was not fair. Watching Cassie eat a cronut shouldn't make him hard.

This was fucked up in so many different ways and Tevin didn't know where to start.

By the time Finley pulled the car into the garage, the cronuts were done.

Thank fucking God.

"We're out in the middle of nowhere, so if you run, we'll find you."

Cassie stared straight ahead, avoiding Tevin's gaze.

"Are you going to behave? Or will we have a repeat of earlier?"

She turned to him while cleaning the sugar from her fingers and his cock jumped to attention. Of course, it did. He wasn't worried what would happen if she decided to make things difficult. Her finger came out of her mouth with a pop as she shrugged.

Fuck him.

"Will I get more cronuts if I behave?"

"Nope. But I won't spank you if you behave."

Cassandra tugged up the boots that all the other mates wore.

Jackson swore they were more comfortable than bedroom slippers, but Tevin didn't buy it.

"Fine."

When any woman used the word fine, they usually meant the exact opposite. From the look Finley shared with Tevin, they both knew he was in for a world of hurt.

"Finley, get the dog."

"I have the bags." Maddie volunteered.

Tevin wrapped his fingers around Cassie's wrist and led her from the car. He wouldn't have put it on a top ten list for the most graceful move, but at least no one would have to chase after her.

They all paused at the door leading to the underground tunnel and waited on Tevin. No one wanted to be the one to open the door and lead someone who might be their enemy inside. In retrospect, he probably should have called ahead and warned Vixen. He pressed his palm against the locking mechanism and the door opened.

Finley, along with the dog, who was smelling every nook and cranny his nose could reach, led the way. Tevin kept his hold on Cassie and led her along behind him with Maddie taking up the rear.

She dragged her feet the entire way, a silent protest that bordered on the misbehaving thing they'd talked about earlier, but still wasn't technically crossing the line.

Or maybe she hoped for another spanking. When his hand landed on her ass earlier, he'd heard the soft moan and it was impossible to ignore the flared scent of her arousal.

There were too many other things to consider at the moment, but Tevin planned on circling back to the subject when the timing was better.

As soon as they reached the armory, Tevin and Finley lost their equipment and gear. All while Tevin kept a careful eye on Cassie. The last thing they needed was for her to sneak one of the weapons. Maddie pushed ahead of them and out the door.

"I'm headed to the kitchen to get some food ready. I don't think I need to be around for your little meeting with Vixen."

"Maybe we could hide her somewhere and Vixen won't find out."

"What?"

"What?"

Both Tevin and Cassie spoke at once.

Finley grinned. "It was just a thought. Too bad Pocket's camper isn't redone. We could have used that."

Tevin rolled his eyes at Finley's commentary. He told himself he didn't care, and for the most part he didn't. What he cared about most was figuring out how to keep Cassie from getting into trouble and Vixen from killing him.

On the brighter side of things, at least he got to see Cassie again.

"We'll figure this out, okay? Remember the whole thing with Danielle's program is we can't say for sure why it's pulling up the information, only that it did." He slapped Tevin's shoulder.

"That can probably wait. There are some other things on the top of the list."

Like what he was going to do about Cassie. Taking her back to Broken Peak was one thing, but then he had to convince her she couldn't leave. At least not until they figured out what role she played and why that loner had been keeping an eye on her. And because there was no way in hell that Cassie would make things easy for him, they'd have to keep her under guard.

They left the armory and headed to Bray's office with the dog trotting happily behind them. Finley stopped at the door and looked over at Tevin.

"Let me go in, okay? We don't have any spare rooms, so I guess bring her to yours."

Shit. Now Finley was covering for him.

"Thanks."

He pulled Cassie along behind him, hoping no one else was in the kitchen except Maddie. Fortunately, things were looking up. Only Maddie was in the kitchen, and she waved them in.

Maybe a quick detour was in order? They would definitely need a drink for the eventual conversation with his Alphas.

Tevin turned into the kitchen, bringing both Cassie and the dog with him. He dropped her wrist as soon as they reached the table and headed to the pantry in the back of the room where they kept the moonshine.

With a jug in hand, he circled around to the cabinets and grabbed four glasses. Finley would probably be on his way after he discovered the empty office. When he turned around, Finley had not only arrived, but was crouched in front of Cassie and helping her take off her boots.

The moment her hand rested on Finley's shoulder to help keep her balance, Tevin growled low. The sight almost drove him to the same level of anger as when Cassie mentioned her boyfriend.

Another thing he'd have to take care of.

He set the glasses on the table and poured everyone a healthy shot of the moonshine.

"Cassie?"

Her head snapped around at the sound of his voice. "What?"

"Sit down over here." He nodded to the empty chair next to him.

She crossed her arms over her chest and glared at him through narrowed eyes. He wanted to kiss away the wrinkles that formed in the corner of her eyes, but that would have to wait.

Finley stood and pressed his hand against the back of her shoulder, giving her a gentle push towards Tevin.

Cassie touching Finley was bad enough, but Finley touching her sent Tevin and his wolf into levels of anger he'd never experienced before.

It didn't make any sense. Finley was happily mated and was being friendly. Except Tevin didn't want anyone else touching her except him. Fuck, no one else except him was going to touch her if he had his way.

He held out a glass of moonshine and nodded to the chair again. "Sit down, please."

"Fine." She shuffled around the table to the chair he nodded to and sat. Lifting the glass to her nose she sniffed it then set it back down. "I don't want that."

"For fuck's sake, Cassie, stop being so damn argumentative." As soon as the words left his mouth, he knew they were the wrong words.

Cassie pulled her lips between her teeth and her chin quivered.

Fuck him, she was going to cry.

He didn't do crying. He couldn't handle it. Not even when Foster, Jackson's four-year-old pup, fell down and hurt himself. When tears fell, Tevin ran.

"Cassie's taking medicine and she can't drink with it." Maddie stood and grabbed a clean glass from the cabinet and a bottle of orange juice from the fridge.

"Why are you on meds? Are you sick? What's wrong?"

Worst-case scenarios invaded his mind.

She was dying. Maybe that was why he hadn't seen her at the Dirty Whistle since that one night. What if she was really sick and dying. Except she didn't look sick. Or act sick. Not if her temper was anything to go by.

Maddie set a glass of orange juice in front of Cassie. "Relax, Tev. It's just some antibiotics."

Cassie was busy sharing a look with Maddie. Like they were communicating in some weird way. Almost the same way Vixen and Bray did.

What the hell? Cassie and Maddie shouldn't be getting along. In fact, she should be hating Maddie as much as she pretended to hate Tevin.

Yeah, that needed to stop. Before she could protest, he scooped her up from her chair and sat back down in it with her in his lap. "Why didn't you tell me you were sick?"

"When should I have told you? When you knocked on my door or when you carried me out of the inn?"

Fuck. He shouldn't have handled her as rough as he had. He pressed her head against his shoulder.

"Tevin, I need to see my doctor."

"Maddie's a doctor. She can take care of you."

"I have a life, Tevin. Things I need to get back to. Plus, my grandma will worry if I don't call her."

Tevin sighed. Her temper was about to skyrocket when he told her she couldn't leave for a while. But maybe he could stall and put that off for a few days. Or better yet, maybe he could get Vixen to tell her.

"We can talk about that later, I want to make sure you're okay." He slid his hands across her cheeks and held her face so she had to look at him. Her eyes widened and he couldn't help himself. He bent his head forward and brushed his lips across hers. "Cassie, I promised I'd never hurt you. Remember? That means keeping you healthy too. So, Maddie will check you out and then tomorrow we'll have a long talk."

His lips found hers again, and he swept his tongue across the seam until her lips parted. While he was busy kissing her, he turned her, so she faced him with her legs straddling his lap.

Fuck. Even in the flannel pants she had on, she was beautiful. And his cock agreed with the sentiment. He was tempted to pick her up and carry her off to his bedroom, strip her bare, and make love to her. But the kiss alone probably pushed her temper. The tantrum he saw in her hotel room was going to be minor compared to the one she would throw if he did any of what he wanted.

She'd have to spend the night in his room, but he wanted to share his bed with her even if they weren't having sex. And that meant playing nice.

Her lips pressed against his, returning his kiss. Just like when they kissed at the bar. If Tevin had his way, no one else would taste those lips except him.

Especially not some asshole of a boyfriend.

Assuming Vixen didn't kill him, Cassie was going to be his, and he didn't plan on letting her go.

Ever.

His wolf was in complete agreement.

CHAPTER ELEVEN

MADDIE sat in Tevin's bedroom with Cassandra. After pushing Tevin out the door, she informed him that she flat out refused to have more than even a social conversation with her if Tevin stayed. He reluctantly agreed to leave them alone, but only when Maddie promised she would come and let him in as soon as she finished the examination.

Between Maddie keeping her secret and taking her oath seriously, some of Cassie's anxiety lessened. Well lessened as much as it could considering Tevin had kidnapped her and brought her to a place filled with shifters if her sense of magic wasn't broken.

It would all make more sense if Tevin had been a creepy stalker with some weird delusions. And for all she knew, he might be a total creeper. Except for the butterflies in her stomach, or maybe it was her magic or her unborn baby, reminding her she didn't actually hate him. And she wasn't frightened of him either. The way he gazed at her. Or how his arms protected her when he held her. Hell, waking up in the morning with his body pressed against her back was amazing.

He'd gotten up with Moose first thing in the morning, after she promised to stay inside the room, and took him outside. Cassandra was slightly concerned when Moose didn't return with him, but Tevin promised no harm would come to her dog either.

And to make things better, he brought her breakfast in bed. Although, that probably had more to do with Tevin wanting to keep her hidden away for a while more. Cassandra still had to meet the rest of the pack. And tell them she knew they were shifters. Oh, and she couldn't forget telling them she was a witch.

"Considering what I found in your bathroom and your sudden appearance at the bar, I'm assuming the pregnancy is recent news?"

Cassandra nodded.

"My specialty was in the emergency room and not prenatal care."

"I don't even know if I am. They were all over the counter tests."

"Yeah, I saw the boxes, but I didn't count them."

"Eight." No point in denying her desire for confirmation. Eight times over.

"Eight boxes?" Maddie's eyes widened at the news.

"Tests."

"Okay, well, we can do a blood test, but I think we both are smart enough to know that eight tests can't all be wrong. The tricky part will be coming up with an excuse for a sonogram, but we don't have to worry about that for a few weeks yet."

"A few weeks?" Cassandra scooted closer to the edge of the bed. "I won't be here in a few weeks, right?"

"Let's take this one day at a time, okay? In the meantime, we'll stick with the antibiotic story." Maddie took a breath. "Have you decided what you're going to do?"

She hadn't told the father of her baby that she was pregnant, but she was about to share with the female who helped kidnap her that she was planning on having the baby.

It was official. Her life could be one of those made for TV movies.

"Assuming I'm still here in a few weeks, plan for a sonogram and whatever else I need to worry about."

Maddie nodded and smiled at her. "Good. As long as you don't have any complications, I can treat you here in the Lodge. And we'll keep things vague for Tevin's benefit. Maybe stick with a bacteria in your intestine? That way we don't have to go into specifics."

She was waiting for Cassandra to agree. And she knew she should, but a tinge of guilt hit her belly. The first person she told should have been Tevin. Not Maddie, even if she was a doctor.

"Don't worry, I'll be surprised when you tell him." Maddie grinned then cocked her head to the side and stared at Cassandra. "I'm assuming the baby's his."

"Yeah, it's his. Ugh, I hate using the word it to describe my unborn baby."

"Well, your baby is about the size of a poppy seed right now."

Cassandra leaned back on her hands and stretched her legs out in front of her. "Really? That small?"

"I'm surprised you didn't spend hours on the internet."

"I only learned yesterday. I mean, I kind of suspected when my period was a few days late, but I waited a week. Just in case."

"That's a good thing. The internet is the bane of any doctor's existence. Well meaning people share a lot of bad information." Maddie smiled and winked at her. "Do you want me to recommend a few books? If you're interested. But all you need to worry about now is taking care of yourself."

"What about soft cheese and fish?"

"If it has mold, then avoid the soft cheese. As for fish, it's fish that have a higher risk of mercury. Salmon, trout, even shrimp should be fine. But fish isn't a big meal here, so you don't have to worry." Maddie reached over and squeezed Cassandra's knee. Reassuring her with a small gesture. "As long as you aren't eating only one thing for every meal, you'll be fine. We've been having babies for eons now, and will continue to have babies. Trust your body. It knows how to take care of you."

It was difficult not to like Maddie. Even if she had been part of Cassandra's kidnapping. She might not specialize in obstetrics, but she was a pleasant doctor.

"What about coffee?" Cassandra already avoided alcohol. Well, for two days. She wasn't sure she'd be able to give up coffee too.

"Okay, so back to the moderation thing. As long as coffee is your only source of caffeine, a small cup should be all right, but that means no chocolate." Maddie sat down on the bed next to Cassandra. "This isn't my specialty, but I can do some research and get some more information for you in a few weeks."

There was the few weeks thing again. What did Maddie know that Cassandra didn't?

Maddie handed Cassandra a small orange bottle. "The label says Cipro, but they're vitamins. Take one each morning."

Cassandra pulled up her knees and hugged them close to her chest. "Thanks."

"You know Tevin's been pacing the hallway if he's not sitting right outside the door." Maddie stood and headed to the door. "Frankly, I'm surprised he hasn't broken down the door."

"We should probably put him out of his misery.

"Cassandra." Maddie turned back and studied her. Like she wanted to say something, but wasn't sure how to say it. "The longer you wait to tell him, the worse it will be. We can pretend you didn't know for maybe another week, but Tevin can count the weeks."

She stared at the ground, not wanting to look at Maddie. "I know."

Maddie accepted her response and opened the bedroom door. Sure enough, Tevin hovered right outside the door and pushed his way past Maddie to get to Cassandra. He sat down next to her and reached for her hand.

"Are you okay?"

It was kind of cute the way he was concerned about her. And, if she thought about it for very long, she'd feel guilty for lying to him. But if he didn't learn she was pregnant for a few days, it wouldn't hurt him. Right?

"Cassandra's fine. Nothing to be worried about." Maddie left before Tevin asked anymore questions.

Smart female. If she didn't have to answer any questions, she didn't have to lie.

Tevin cupped Cassandra's cheeks and lifted her face, so she looked in his eyes. "Promise me everything's okay?"

"I swear."

"And if you feel worse, you'll let me know?"

She should have told him then. It would have been a sweet moment, and he'd probably be fine. Or at least the male sitting with her would be fine. The one who got all growly when she mentioned a boyfriend might not be thrilled with her decision not to tell him right away.

"Promise." She bit down hard on cheek.

"Okay. Lunch is ready. Once we finish eating, we're going to have our talk."

Ugh, the talk. She'd been so worried about her visit with Maddie she was able to push the shifter and witch thing to the back of her mind. How could she bring up the whole supernatural thing?

She needed to talk with her grandma. Memaw would know what to do. But first she needed access to a phone and before that there would be the appointed talk.

Tevin wrapped his hand around hers and pulled her to her feet. "I hope you like soup and sandwiches. We tend to have it for lunch a lot because it's easier to feed us all."

They walked down the hallway to the kitchen and Cassandra took a deep breath. It was the time of reckoning. She expected the room to be filled with shifters, but no one else was in the room. Not even Finley.

However, sitting in the middle of the large table was a huge plate of cronuts. He must have asked someone to go to town to get them. Which wasn't a small feat, considering they lived nearly an hour from War.

Tevin pointed her to a chair then sat down next to her.

"So, I think it's tomato soup and BLTs. But if you don't want a BLT, I can make something else for you."

"A BLT is fine." Although she was tempted to forgo the sandwich and start with dessert. The Cronuts looked better than the ones she had last night.

Tevin stacked three sandwiches on her plate then ladled the soup into a large bowl. "So, I'm going to have to run a quick errand after we have our talk."

The conversation was forced. Like he wasn't saying what he wanted to say.

"You want me to behave?"

"It's more than wanting, Cassie." Tevin bit into his sandwich, leaving the rest of the sentence unsaid.

"What errand?" Two could play the forced conversation game.

"Nothing big, just some responsibilities I have to take care of."

She rolled her eyes and bit into the sandwich. As much as Tevin liked telling her she should trust him, he didn't reciprocate. The crisp bacon tasted good and she took another large bite.

"Cassie."

After she took another large bite, she looked over at him. She must have had a crumb or something in the corner of her mouth, because Tevin saw it. He reached out and brushed his thumb over the spot then brought it to his mouth and licked it off.

Her imagination took off as she watched him. All she could think of was the naughty place his tongue could visit. She grabbed the glass of juice and finished its contents in a few swallows.

"Cassie, when I leave, you need to promise me you won't snoop around. Okay?" He bit into his own sandwich.

His tone was the same as the night before when he threw her over his shoulder. The message was clear. Either she behaved or she wouldn't be sitting down for at least a week.

CHAPTER TWELVE

TEVIN walked along the path to Mac's cabin. The old coyote shifter was a close ally of the Broken Peak Pack and had involved himself in the pack's life. Normally he liked visiting with Mac, but the last place he wanted to be was sitting in Mac's cabin with Vixen and Bray.

First Tevin would have to explain that he'd taken the initiative to check out the Voisin contact discovered from the target Vixen sent him after. Then he'd need to tell them exactly why he brought Cassie back to Broken Peak with him when he found her instead of leaving her in her hotel room.

He arrived earlier than Bray said he should be at Mac's, mostly because he figured getting over the explanation a bit sooner would make his punishment easier to deal with.

Best result would be added patrols. Worst result would be Gareth cleaning up his dead body. He wondered if Finley would tell Cassie that Tevin left town and wasn't coming back.

As he neared the cabin, he saw Maddie talking with Vixen on the front porch. She hadn't said anything about seeing Vixen. If he hadn't been on as many patrols with her as he had, he might have worried what she was sharing with Vixen. Except he was more worried that she hadn't mentioned she was stopping by Mac's than *why* Maddie was there.

When she turned her head and looked in his direction with a slight look of surprise on her face, Tevin inched closer to worrying. But she said something to Vixen and walked down the porch steps and directly to Tevin.

"I didn't know you had a meeting with Vixen?"

"I needed to swing by Mac's and Vixen was here. Not a meeting." Maddie tucked her hands into her front pockets. "So, how'd the talk go."

"Honestly? Better than I expected."

"I was wondering if you'd have some bruises." Maddie grinned. "How much did you tell her?"

"That someone was interested in us, and they mentioned her. I didn't cover the details, but she probably suspects we did something to the male. If we can get the local paper to run the suicide story, she might buy it."

"Look, Tevin..."

"Hey, do me a favor? Keep her safe. Finley said he would, but you're probably better equipped for it. I promised her I wouldn't hurt her and I meant. But if something happens to me, I need you to keep my promise."

"Don't be so dramatic. Nothing is going to happen."

Tevin was tempted to believe her, but Vixen and Bray didn't like people showing up in pack territory. Much less being brought into the Lodge by a pack member. Everyone who showed up had ultimately been invited. And Cassie definitely hadn't been invited.

"Just promise."

"Fine, yeah, whatever. But seriously, nothing is going to happen to you so you can keep your promise to her."

Tevin nodded, not trusting his mouth to form words that made any sense. He looked over Maddie's shoulder at Mac's cabin. Vixen was still on the porch and was looking at him. He needed to get the fucking meeting over with. At least now he knew Cassie would be taken care of. That made things easier.

"What about the other thing, like you and almost everyone else at Broken Peak being shifters? What did you tell her."

"Skipped that part."

"She didn't ask why you're living out in the middle of nowhere. In a cabin built into a mountain. With an armory."

"I'm hoping she thinks we're survivalists."

"She bought what you did share with her?"

"Yeah, it was the truth. Not the whole truth. Plus, she didn't ask any questions. So, I think we're at the I'm going to pretend I told her everything, and she's going to pretend I told her everything."

"You know that's going to backfire when she's still here in a few weeks. She thinks she's going to leave in a day."

"I'll figure it out when it happens." Tevin glanced over at Vixen. He needed to get over to Vixen or his punishment would be a lot worse. "Hey, I left her alone at the Lodge. Mind swinging by--"

"Alone? Like all alone? Are you crazy?" Maddie sprinted past him then broke into a flat-out run.

Tevin watched her race away before turning back to Vixen. He still didn't know what Maddie and Vixen were talking about or why Maddie was so confident everything would be okay. However, he wished he had a small fraction of her confidence as he walked up the porch steps.

Vixen tilted her head toward the door.

It was time to pay the piper.

CHAPTER THIRTEEN

CASSANDRA sat on the bed and stared at the closed door. Tevin hadn't locked her in, but he might as well have. He threatened every possible punishment he could think of if she went off and explored on her own.

At least she had Moose to keep her company. Except the dog hadn't been very good company because he spent most of his time whining at the door, wanting out. He didn't have to go to the bathroom or anything like that. No, he was whining because Tevin left.

Between their talk and her visit with Maddie, Cassandra decided she wasn't going to spend her time thinking about Tevin. She wasn't doing a very good job of it.

Not knowing how long she had before Tevin came back, she ran through her options. Stay in the room and play the perfect little involuntary house guest. Explore the house she was in. Or explore outside. She figured as long as she stayed close to the house, he couldn't say she was misbehaving.

But she also needed a phone. If she wanted to talk with her grandma, a phone was the only way to do it. Without having a pantry full of ingredients, she couldn't use a scrying bowl to speak with Memaw. That left a phone.

She thought she saw Finley with one, so that probably meant others had one as well. And even though she hadn't seen Tevin with one, she knew if he had one, it would be on him. No way would he trust her not to snoop through his room.

Looking over at Moose she narrowed her eyes at the noisy beast. "You up for a little subterfuge, Moo?"

The dog wagged his tail. Of course, he did. His tail never stopped wagging.

"Okay, I need you to run off. Can you do that for me, Moose? Just run down the hallway." She might have called a bit of magic to give him a nudge. She figured there wouldn't be any kick back since wanting to keep her grandma from worrying wasn't selfish. Plus, the reason she wanted to call was for the poppy seed, as she started calling her unborn child. There was no way the magic would decide she was being selfish. It wasn't like she was using her magic to bring a phone to her.

Although...

No. That would definitely fall to the selfish side of the scale. But she could add to Moose's nudge. Maybe have him run towards a phone?

That would totally work. As long as she kept things simple, the magic could usually figure things out on its own. It was only when she added layers to a spell that the magic tended to get confused.

Staring at Moose, she called to the earth's power, pulling it closer to her. When a smallish bundle of magic pulsed in front of her, she whispered her need to it then sent it on its way to Moose.

Her dog usually hated it when she cast spells. Probably because it changed the currents and flows of magic the earth naturally created. Except this time, he didn't seem to mind. It was almost like Moose was excited for the magic.

As soon as she felt the magic wrap and twist itself around Moose, she hopped to her feet and opened the door. "Go on, buddy."

And Moose was off. Tail wagging, paws loping over the floor, straight down the hallway with Cassandra right behind him.

Instead of yelling and calling attention to herself, she used an angry whisper. In case someone caught her in mid heist, she'd have a reasonable excuse and the angry whisper only helped with the facade.

They passed several closed doors, the kitchen, and more closed doors. She hoped the magic knew where it was leading Moose. The dog made a sharp left turn and almost lost his footing. His paws scrambled over the hardwood floor, but he didn't spin out. He pushed his way into a room, one where the door hadn't been closed all the way, and jumped around in happy circles.

Cassandra was right behind him with a similar skid to a halt as soon as she entered the room.

"Holy crap." She let out a long breath. Where the fuck was she?

Computer screens took up most of the surface area of the room and the computers they belonged to took up nearly three quarters of the floor. What was this place? She glanced at a screen and had to look again to make sure she saw things correctly.

The top line of the screen closest to her had her phone number followed by several more numbers. She had no idea what the other numbers meant. But what she did know was that her number being on the computer was not a coincidence.

Moose bit at the air and yipped.

Shit. The phone. She could figure out why her phone number showed up on the screen later, but for now she needed a phone.

Ignoring the screens, she scanned the tables and walls, hoping to find a phone. Nothing. No phone.

Crap.

Why would the magic bring her here if there wasn't a phone? Unless it confused phone with her phone number. No. She didn't think the magic could read a computer screen.

Moose hopped up and down near one of the two chairs in the room. Cassandra eyed him for a moment before looking at the chair.

What do you know? A phone. If someone left a phone here, on a chair, they probably left it everywhere. Which meant it could easily be misplaced.

Cassandra snatched the phone and tucked it into the waist of her pants and hidden with her shirt. "Come on, Moose, let's go for a walk."

The w-word sent him into a fresh tizzy. He led her out of the computer room, back down the hallway to the kitchen, where he turned right then ran up the hallway to the front door. All without a lick of magic. Thank God he remembered where to go since Cassandra hadn't been anywhere except the kitchen, Tevin's room, and now the computer room.

The front room was huge. Like the massive reception area of a ski lodge without any reception desks. Couches and chairs filled the room, but Cassandra couldn't find a TV. Interesting. She figured males like Tevin and Finley would have the latest video game console and a massive flat screen TV to play the games on.

Before the decor of the room distracted her further, she opened the door and let Moose outside. He happily raced down the steps and around the yard, marking almost everything.

Cassandra needed to get to the edge of the yard. Preferably far enough away from the house to not be seen, but not too far, so she looked suspicious.

"Come on, Moose, let's take a stroll."

She headed towards her left. The yard to her right appeared to have the most traffic. Which made sense, since it was right in front of the porch. But the large open space to the left looked less used. As much as she wanted to look around and study the landscape, she didn't want to waste any precious time she had with the phone.

Moose roamed around, but stayed close enough to keep her in sight and always ran back to her. Like he was checking on her. When she determined that she was far enough away from the house and also conveniently in the shadow of a tree, she pulled the phone out.

Crap.

The screen was locked. Of course, it was. And it probably used something more than a password. Maybe a fingerprint too.

She'd have to use magic again. Focusing her need on keeping her grandma from worrying, she once more called the magic to her. As the magic swarmed around her, she sent a thin stream to the phone. A few seconds later and the screen came to life, as though it had never been locked.

With a grateful thanks, she sent the magic away. She wasn't sure if shifters could read earth magic, but if they could, they wouldn't ignore two uses in a short time frame.

Before the phone could re lock itself, she quickly dialed her grandma's number. The phone rang three times before her grandma picked up.

"Memaw?"

"Cassandra? What's wrong?"

"Memaw, I'm at Broken Peak and I have a problem."

"What? You're where? Cassandra, listen to me carefully and do exactly what I tell you to."

"Memaw, I have a problem and I need to talk to you about it and I don't have much time."

Her grandma's normally gentle voice turned sharp. "Cassandra Voisin, we can discuss your problem later. But right now you need to listen to me. You're outside right?"

"Yeah, how did you know?"

"The Book. Now listen. You're going to throw the phone as hard as you can into the woods, and put as much magic as you can behind it. Then you are going to turn around and run back to the Lodge. Once inside, you are going to lock the door. I don't care who's knocking on it, you don't let them in. Even if it's the pack Alphas."

"Pack?" All Cassandra knew was that Broken Peak was filled with shifters, she didn't know what kind. How did her grandma know it was a pack living in Broken Peak?

"Later. Now throw the phone girl and run." The line went dead.

Cassandra hesitated all of thirty seconds to throw the phone, but it was enough. She sensed the shifter magic before she saw it. And the shifter wasn't in his human form.

Holy crap.

A mammoth hyena stepped out from the forest and headed towards her. This wasn't a run-of-the-mill hyena someone might see in a zoo. It was at least three times the size of its natural counterpart.

There was no way she'd be able to outrun it.

Moose stepped in front of her with his hackles raised and released a low growl.

The hyena could have bitten Moose in half if he wanted to. And from the way he stalked towards them, the hyena planned on doing exactly that.

A high-pitched scream came from behind Cassandra, but no way was she turning her back on the hyena. She had never used magic as a weapon, but she wasn't letting the shifter hurt Moose, herself, or the poppy seed. There was a first time for everything. She hoped the magic understood that self-preservation was not at all the same as selfishness.

The scream came again. This time closer. But still, Cassandra didn't turn her back.

She called the magic to her with an urgent cry and not the gentle beckoning her grandma had taught her. And the magic responded. In Waves. It rushed to her, swirling around her and wrapping itself within and around her. An electrical charge swept over her, hovering above her skin. As though it didn't want to touch her.

Never before had she felt this much power. And frankly, she hoped to never feel it again. The excited magic wasn't playful, it was agitated.

She might as well have put up a sixty-five-foot billboard with the words 'Magic being used' right next to her. Even the non supernaturals would feel something in the air.

The hyena took another step towards her.

Another scream from behind her immediately followed.

Moose stepped back until his bottom pressed against her legs.

Offense or defense?

Cassandra had to decide and fast. Splitting the magic would defeat the purpose of calling as much as she had. The approach needed to be all or nothing.

Magic used offensively was dangerous. That had been one of the first lessons she learned. Once magic had a taste for harm, it would seek it out. She couldn't be the cause of tainting so much magic. She *wouldn't* be the cause.

Defense it would be. A protective spell that would keep the hyena away from her and keep her alive. Maybe a shield? She'd done shield spells before, but never on herself or another person.

It looked like today was going to be a first for a lot of things.

Just before she released the magic to do her will, the image of a poppy seed came to her mind. And in that one instant, she changed her mind.

No way would that bastard harm her and Tevin's baby. She wouldn't allow it.

With more force than she knew she had, Cassandra threw the gathered magic directly at the hyena shifter.

CHAPTER FOURTEEN

"CASSANDRA!"

She opened her eyes at the shouting, but didn't recognize anything around her. Not that there was anything to recognize. Everything around her was gone. The trees. The grass. The sun. The entire world was gone.

Empty black space surrounded her. Cassandra sat up. Or at least she thought she sat up. Her body sort of floated around in the nothingness.

Where the hell was she?

"Cassandra, open your eyes."

There was that voice again. Coming from somewhere outside the space. She recognized the voice. It belonged to someone she knew. Or she should know. But her mind couldn't come up with a name.

"Cassandra, it's Maddie. I need you to open your eyes."

Ah, Maddie. The nice doctor shifter who kept Cassandra's secret.

Everything from the last few minutes flooded back into Cassandra's memory.

Calling the magic to her then sending it at the hyena. She didn't remember exactly what happened to the hyena shifter, but one second he was there and the next flecks and specks of ash fluttered to the ground.

Crap!

Cassandra had destroyed another life. She had used magic the way it was never to be used. Ever. No matter what.

And the void must be what happened when you used magic for the wrong reasons.

Holy crap!

She could have destroyed Maddie too.

Not that Maddie didn't deserve a little uncomfortable in her life for taking part in the kidnapping scheme, but she didn't deserve complete and total destruction.

The idea of destroying Maddie sent Cassandra to her knees. Well, as much as she could be on her knees floating around in a void.

The void shook.

Okay, so maybe the void itself wasn't the punishment. Maybe it was what came after the void?

"Wake up, Cassandra. Open your eyes for me." There was Maddie's voice again. But how could it reach through into the void? "I promised Tevin I would keep you safe. We don't break promises and I don't plan on starting now. So you need to wake up."

Her head hurt thinking about it.

"Oh God, Maddie. What did I do?"

"Cassandra? Are you okay? I can hear your voice. What's wrong?" The void shook again. "What happened? Did that shifter do something?"

Holy hell. Maddie's voice took on a tone similar to Tevin's when she mentioned the hypothetical boyfriend.

"No."

"What question are you answering, Cassandra? The being okay or the shifter hurting you."

"Um, I don't know if I'm okay and no, I don't think he hurt me."

And how the hell were they having a conversation with her in a void? Cassandra couldn't see Maddie. Well, she couldn't see anything.

"Um both?"

Maddie cursed up a storm. Every curse word Cassandra had heard and some she hadn't ever heard echoed around her. The void rattled again.

She blinked her eyes several times and took a quick inventory of her body. She could move everything without any pains. Then again, she was also floating around in nothingness, so maybe things didn't hurt the same way they did in the world.

"I think I'm okay. As far as I can tell nothing is hurt."

"Okay. Where are you?"

"I don't know."

"What do you mean you don't know?"

"Just that."

"Well look around and tell me what you see."

"Nothing."

"How can there be nothing?"

"I don't know, but there is. It's black and I'm all floaty. And we're having a conversation, which is freaking me the hell out."

"Yeah, it's fucking with me too, but I'm doing my best to ignore it for the time being."

"Um, Maddie?"

"Yeah?"

"Are you hurt? Did I hurt you?"

"What? No. I'm fine. There was a huge flash of light, something I've never seen before, and let's face it, I don't think I want to see it again. I closed my eyes and when I opened them you were lying on the ground. Well, are lying on the ground. I'm looking at your body right now."

"So, um, I guess my real secret is out. And so is yours."

"Let's put that down as something we'll talk about later, because right now I have enough shit on my plate that's giving me the heebie jeebies."

Cassandra silently agreed.

Wait. The phone. "Maddie. Is there a phone somewhere around me?"

"Yeah?"

"Is it still unlocked?"

Please let it be unlocked.

Cassandra had never been one to pray before. She thanked the earth for its gifts and revered it, but the praying thing always felt odd. Right now, it wasn't odd at all. It was the right thing to do.

She begged the source of the magic swirling around to intervene.

"It's unlocked."

Well, what did you know? Praying worked.

"Dial the last number. It's my grandma."

Maddie didn't ask any questions, which Cassandra figured was a good thing. She couldn't see what was happening, so she hoped that Maddie was busy dialing.

"Cassandra!" Memaw's voice swirled into the void and surrounded Cassandra in a warm embrace. "Is everything okay? Why are you calling."

"Memaw, I'm here!"

"Um, Cassandra's grandma, I'm Maddie. She says she's here."

"I can hear her just fine." Memaw's no nonsense voice eased Cassandra's anxiety. "Tell me exactly what happened and what's happening. The Book is being a twat waffle."

"Memaw!"

"Well it is. It's not saying anything. The writing on the page disappeared. It's never done that before. Either you changed things or..."

"Or? Or what? Memaw, you can't leave off a sentence like that."

"Or we aren't supposed to know and I'm not sure which is worse." Memaw shifted gears. "Maddie, dear, my granddaughter isn't much help right now, so I need you to tell me what happened."

"There was a threat."

"I know that part. Fast forward to why you're calling."

"Her body's here with me, but she's not."

"Oh."

Well, that was one way to put it. "I'm inside a kind of void, Memaw. There's nothing here."

"And how did you get in there?" The announcement didn't faze her grandma in the slightest.

"I don't know, I woke up here."

"What did you do right before you woke up wherever you're at?"

"You don't know about it?" Her grandma's words dashed whatever hopes Cassandra had that Memaw could help.

"No, because *I* followed The Book's directions. So tell me what happened."

"There was a flash of light. And, well shit, I'm a shifter, and I was shifted right when it happened. As soon as the burst of light happened, I shifted back, but not because I willed it. It wasn't even like when the clan Chiefs force shifts. Then Cassandra was lying on the ground. It's like she's unconscious. She has a pulse and her breathing is fine, but she's not here. And when she talks, I can hear her voice all around me."

Silence hung in the air when Maddie finished her explanation.

Finally, after what felt like an eternity, Memaw spoke. But it wasn't the voice of her grandma coming through the void. The voice belonged to Sybil Voisin, the matriarch of the Voisins and the most revered of all the witches.

"You pulled shifter magic? You used the moon's magic along with the earth's?"

"Um, I don't know. Maybe?"

The memory of the one and only time Cassandra had used her magic outside with witnesses came to mind. Memaw had been both angry and proud. Angry that she had to clean up after Cassandra's blunder, but proud of the magic Cassandra had wielded.

"There's no maybe about it. You did. The last record of anyone using disciplines that didn't belong to them happened thousands of years ago during the Great Battle and the reason you went to War."

"Memaw, can we dispense with that silly legend and focus on what's happening now?"

"What's happening now is because of that silly legend, as you call it. So let's dispense with calling it a silly legend."

Maddie cleared her throat. Cassandra didn't blame her. Listening to the Voisin women bicker couldn't have been an enjoyable experience.

"Fine." Cassandra reluctantly agreed.

"There's only one being who might be able to help. He's a bit of a dick nozzle though."

"Memaw!"

"Well, he is. He's made my life miserable. And if you want to blame anyone for you going to War, blame him. This is all his fault."

This is all your fault.

The words danced around Cassandra's mind. She said those words just over a month ago. And the man she told them to agreed with her.

"Alexander." All three women spoke at once.

"The only problem is I have no way of contacting him."

"I can," Maddie said.

"Well, what are you waiting for?" Memaw's crisp tone returned with a vengeance.

Cassandra guessed that Maddie was calling Alex because there was another long pause.

"Um, Memaw?" Cassandra figured since Maddie was busy, now was as good of a time as any to let her grandma know the reason why Cassandra had called in the first place. "It turns out witches and shifters can have babies. I'm pregnant."

"Talk about burying the lede."

"Yeah. It was why I was calling you, but then everything went pear-shaped."

"Okay, Alexander's coming." Maddie interrupted.

"He is?" Memaw's voice sounded surprised. "That man has never once come when I wanted him to. But he did have a knack for showing up when he was the last one I wanted to see."

"Glad to hear you too, Sybil."

Holy crap. He was here. And not here as in the world, but here in the void with Cassandra.

"I spent more time in here than I care to admit, Cassandra, especially when I share how to get out of it."

"Where am I?"

"Where magic lives. Or is made. I don't know exactly." Alexander smiled at her and reached for her hand. "I've been waiting a long time for you."

Cassandra took his hand. For the first time since everything had happened. Arriving at War, the one night stand with Tevin, finding out she was pregnant, the kidnapping, and then the whole using her magic against another being, Cassandra felt at ease. It was as though every-thing was right in the world.

"Ask the magic to let you out. Tell it you want to leave." Alexander leaned in and whispered in her ear.

"What?" Cassandra couldn't have possibly heard him right.

"What? What did he say?" Memaw asked with a sharp tone. "What are you telling my granddaughter, Alexander?"

"Don't worry, Sybil. I'm not sharing any of your secrets." Alexander chuckled. "Just ask, Cassandra."

So she did. In the same way she asked the magic to help her find a phone and when she called it to help with the hyena, she closed her eyes and asked the magic to let her out.

It didn't work. She felt nothing. No magic. No electrical charge. Nothing that let her know the magic listened to her.

Cassandra opened her eyes and turned to Alexander.

Instead of the blackness surrounding her, she was back in the world. The brown grass pricked at her skin, and the sun shined down on her. The tree, the one with the shadow she had used to hide, loomed above her. Moose licked her face. Maddie smiled down at her. She felt every-thing, even the crisp March air.

"What happened?" Memaw asked. "Did it work?"

"Yeah, it worked." Cassandra sat up and bent her head back until the sun graced her face with its heat.

For a while, she thought she'd never see the sun again.

"Thank you, Alexander."

Except he wasn't there. She looked around the area thinking he had stepped away, but he was nowhere in sight.

"He's not here." Maddie said.

"Why not?"

"Probably because he can't be." Memaw answered.

"What do you mean?" Cassandra asked.

"I'm sure you'll see him again and he'll explain it to you."

Cassandra turned and threw her arms around Maddie. Maddie returned the hug. Even Moose got into it and licked at their faces, not wanting to be left out.

"It's okay," Maddie said.

"No it's not. I almost hurt you. I could have hurt you."

"How could you hurt me?"

"That magic. It was uncontrolled and more power than I've ever called before. I know Tevin said not to snoop, but I needed to call my memaw. The whole shifter and witch thing was an unknown and I didn't know what you knew and what I could or should tell you. And then the hyena shifter showed up. I meant to call a shield. Something to protect me, but at the last minute I thought about the poppy seed. And I sent the magic at the hyena." The words spilled from her mouth before she could stop them.

"If I'd known that Tevin was going to leave you alone, I would have been here. Or made sure someone else was here with you."

"But why do I need anyone with me? Oh, God, I want to go home."

"You are sweetheart. I know it doesn't make any sense yet, but we need to trust The Book." Memaw's soft voice came from the phone. "Now, we've solved the current problem of getting you out of wherever you were. It's time you do what I told you to and go inside. I love you, Cassandra, and I'll see you soon."

Memaw ended the call and the line went dead.

"Come on, let's do what your grandma suggested and get inside." Maddie pulled Cassandra to her feet and led her across the lawn to the house built into the mountain.

Now that she looked at it from the outside, Cassandra saw it for the fortress it was. The only way in was through the front, but the open yard made it impossible to not be seen. And even though the house might have appeared to be built directly in front of the wall of stone behind it, she knew how far back the house actually went.

"I have a present for you." Maddie's words broke through Cassandra's wandering thoughts.

"More cronuts?" She was on to their trick, but she didn't care. Although, she wasn't sure what was worse, that she could be so easily bribed by the delicacy or that they used it to bribe her.

"Nope, but I can get my cousin to pick up some after her shift." Maddie laughed as she opened the front door.

They walked into the front room. Moose pushed his way between their legs, then hopped on a couch and bounced around the cushions. Maddie led her to a chair with two bags sitting on it. A line drawing of a pregnant woman graced the side of the bag.

"Pregnancy clothes?"

"I talked to a friend who called in a favor. Supposedly these are the hot new thing. They're meant to grow with you and don't actually look like maternity wear."

"I need to tell him."

"Yeah. But I know why you haven't."

"You do?"

"Of course. We've all hidden things as a way of punishment. Hell, I think Vixen is the queen of keeping secrets from Bray when he does something that really pisses her off."

"You won't tell him?"

"No. But at some point he's going to figure it out and if you end up completely chickening out, then I might have to tell him. I like you, Cassandra, but Tevin's my friend too."

Cassandra didn't say anything. She reached inside the bags and pulled out the clothes. Everything was a knit fabric that would stretch with her body as it grew. And there were a lot of items. Leggings, camisoles, long-sleeved shirts, skirts, cardigans, even a dress. Everything was black, except for a shirt and a camisole, those two items were white.

While she admired the clothing, Maddie took the bags and crumpled them up, hiding the image on the side. "Cassandra. Like your grandma said, you can't go home. And you can't go back to the hotel."

She closed her eyes. As much as she knew she couldn't, accepting the truth of the words hadn't quite happened yet. "Yeah, Memaw made that clear."

"Alexander can't keep you safe. At least not the same way Tevin will." Maddie sat down in the chair that held the bags.

"Is this like Stockholm Syndrome? You're being nice to me, so I'll want to stay?"

"No. I'm hoping Tevin will pull his head out of his ass." Maddie stretched out her legs. "I've been at the Dirty Whistle almost every night, and Tevin's been there too. Since you, he hasn't been with anyone else."

"Why are you telling me this?" Cassandra balled up the clothes and hugged them to her.

"He didn't tell us to say we didn't know him because he doesn't want to see you."

During the past month, Cassandra had dressed with the intention of going back to the Dirty Whistle more times than she wanted to count. And every time, she chickened out. She had wanted to see Tevin again, but she was more scared that she'd see him with someone else.

"Really?"

"Yeah. Let's hide your new clothes with your things. Tevin and the others will be back soon."

Maddie stood and headed down the hallway, not waiting for Cassandra to follow.

"Maddie?"

"Yeah?"

"Thanks."

"Anytime."

CHAPTER FIFTEEN

NOTHING made sense. In the middle of the meeting with Vixen and Bray, one where neither of them had been angry with Tevin, he'd felt his wolf fade for a minute. One second his wolf was lurking, listening in on the meeting, and the next he was gone.

As suddenly as his wolf disappeared, he was back. Just as confused as Tevin. He wasn't the only one who experienced it either. Everyone stopped talking and stared at one another, but it was Mac who finally spoke, and he only said two words.

"Witch's magic."

So, not only were Vixen and Bray not angry with him, surprised, but not angry, but there were witches in the world? And they had magic? Magic that Mac knew about?

Vixen jumped to her feet and ran out the door.

Bray looked over at Tevin, just as surprised, but quickly followed his mate.

"Well, what are you waiting for, boy? An engraved invitation? Git yer ass out there." Mac waved Tevin out the door.

No fucking sense.

As he ran through the woods, following behind his Alphas, he replayed the meeting.

From walking up the porch, to Vixen's secret smile and Bray's knowing smirk. Vixen hinted that she'd expected the complication, but not the result. Then she praised him for handling the assignment. Vixen didn't praise. She gave begrudging acknowledgments, but not praise.

Bray told Tevin he'd figure out what needed to be done and let them know what he decided.

The whole meeting was surreal. And that was before the witch's magic shit happened. It was like something had taken over Vixen and Bray. They weren't upset that he'd brought Cassie back to the Lodge. In fact, they might have even been cheerful at the news.

And Vixen wasn't ever cheerful, except when Foster was around. She liked kids, though she said she didn't want to be a mom. And she hinted to the mates that the Lodge needed more pups all the time.

She hadn't been like that until Halloween with Foster. She used to help run the pack like a small army. And she was tough as fuck. But after they all went trick-or-treating, she softened.

Tevin was the last of the pack without a mate. No one had pressured him about it, but they didn't have to. He thought about it all the time.

Shit, even her answer when he asked why Maddie was there had been weird. Vixen gave him the exact same answer Maddie had.

Fuck, the entire conversation had been weird. Vixen spoke in circles, like she was telling him something without actually saying it. And it wasn't like she used a bunch of euphemisms either.

Tevin couldn't read any of the fucking signs. Bray told him not to worry about it, but he wasn't sure if that meant not to worry or to worry and fix it.

Then, just before the witch's magic thing happened Bray said the weirdest thing. "I don't worry about you, Tevin. When it comes to the pack, I never have and I never will. But I do worry that the pack will be all there is and that's no way to live. The others might not always put the pack first, not the way you do, and we're grateful for that. More than you'll ever know. But I wouldn't give up any of you."

He got real quiet and looked over at Vixen. "Same goes for Vi. Life without her wouldn't be worth living."

What the fuck kind of meeting was that? He expected a conversation about what happened the night before and to go over the details, but Bray and Vixen sped through that part and got all sappy.

Tevin normally enjoyed it when Bray slipped into giving fatherly advice, but this was fucking weird on so many levels.

He ran into the yard, right behind Bray. Nothing was there, at least not that he could see. But something was off. Like ozone in the air before a thunderstorm.

Shit. Cassie was here. At least, assuming she'd listened to him, she hadn't ventured outside. She was waiting inside for him, but he couldn't decide whether to go inside and find her or to follow his Alphas.

Cassie should hate him. Bringing her to Broken Peak and the middle of danger and giving her a half-assed story. She should hate him, but she hadn't yelled at him since the night before. And everything else he'd thrown at her hadn't made her so much as flinch.

He looked across the yard at his Alphas, standing side-by-side staring at a spot on the ground.

Cassie deserved better than Tevin. She deserved what Bray and Vixen had. Decision made, he turned to the Lodge. He needed to see her and know she was safe.

Tevin should have been paying attention. He shouldn't have stood at the edge of the woods alone, especially after they felt what Mac called Witch's magic. He should have done a lot of things differently. But hindsight could be a bitch, always saying what you did wrong when it's too late to change anything.

"Silly wolf."

Tevin spun toward the voice. What the fuck? Whoever the man was standing there, he wasn't a shifter. But he wasn't human either, at least not in the way that Vixen hadn't been human. Something was off with the man and Tevin couldn't place it.

"Got nothing to say, wolf man?"

Tevin narrowed his eyes at the man. Without any weapons, his only option was to shift. The problem was he didn't know what the man was standing there and if he had enough time to shift. Or why Vixen and Bray hadn't noticed.

The man grinned. "The witch you're hiding got lucky, but you won't."

Witch? What the fuck?

The man stepped toward Tevin in the way of someone who wanted to intimidate someone, but not threaten them. That step decided everything.

Tevin shifted, letting his wolf free while leaping through the air at the man. Except he landed on nothing.

Mocking laughter came from his left, and Tevin spun on his four legs to face the source of the sound.

His wolf didn't pounce, learning his lesson from before. But he did growl, baring his teeth at the stranger.

One slow step at a time forward, the wolf stalked his prey.

"Tevin?" Mac's voice cut through Tevin's and his wolf's rage. The same rage Tevin felt when Cassie mentioned her boyfriend.

His wolf growled, salivating for the chance to tear the stranger's throat out.

The stranger's mouth split into a wider grin, a gross caricature of a smile complete with spittle dripping from the corners of his lips.

What the fuck?

The man had to have been crazy and Tevin and his wolf needed to keep the stranger away from Cassie. They needed to keep her safe.

Mac's hand rested on Tevin's withers, holding him steady. Mac didn't need to, but Tevin appreciated the gesture. The wolf backed up, without any urging from Tevin.

"Tevin? What's going on?"

Mac's question hit Tevin and his wolf like a bag of cement.

The stranger cackled. "Yes, Tevin, what's going on?"

The wolf lunged and the man disappeared. Again. But this time he didn't reappear.

What. The. Fuck.

Tevin urged his wolf to cede control and shifted back without any protest. As soon as his wolf was tucked safely inside, he pulled his clothes back on while he stared at Mac.

"You didn't see that?"

"See what?"

"A man. There was a man here."

Mac shook his head slowly from side to side. "Not saying I don't believe you, but I didn't see anything. Or smell anything."

"I didn't smell anything either." He glanced over at his Alphas, who hadn't moved from the place they were standing. "Neither did they."

That last bit of knowledge rested uneasily on Tevin's shoulders. Vixen's griffin should have let her know something was off, but as far as Tevin could tell, she hadn't even looked back when he shifted.

Tevin stared at the front door of the Lodge. The only thing keeping whatever was out there from getting to Cassie.

Maddie stepped outside and stood on the porch, staring across the lawn at Tevin and Mac.

"Come on." Mac urged Tevin along with him as he headed toward the Lodge.

As soon as they got close, Maddie stepped down from the porch.

"Everything okay?" She asked.

"What happened?" Tevin asked at the same time.

"Cassandra had a spooky moment. She went outside, but stayed in the yard." Maddie added that last bit before Tevin lost his shit.

"Where is she? I need to see her." It hadn't been a few hours, but it felt like weeks since he'd last seen her. Tevin went to push past Maddie, but she stopped him.

"A hyena shifter showed up, and before you wig out, I was there and ready to intervene, but she handled it."

"She handled it?" Tevin's brain couldn't comprehend how Cassie could have handled a shifter. Hell, he didn't want to think about it. "And how come none of the alarms went off?"

"No idea on the alarms, but, um, Tevin, you probably should sit down for this."

His mind was completely focused on Cassie that he didn't hear Maddie's words.

"If a shifter showed up, then... Shit, I can't let her leave Broken Peak." Tevin pressed his palm against his face.

He didn't mean he couldn't let her leave because it was a risk to the Broken Peak pack. Tevin meant he couldn't let her leave. One month without her was more than he could handle and it didn't keep her safe at all. Destiny or fate or whatever the fuck it was might have been a bitch, but something good came from it. He didn't have a reason to stay away from Cassie anymore.

"Cassandra knows that. I don't think she's thrilled with it, but she understands it better than she did before."

"She's going to hate me for this."

"She doesn't hate you and she won't hate you. If she hated you, she'd never have shown up at the Dirty Whistle yesterday. And um, I also don't think getting her out of the hotel would have been as easy as it was."

"What the fuck are you talking about Maddie?"

She opened her mouth to answer, but the front door opened and Cassie stepped out onto the porch. When he'd left her earlier that day, she'd been dressed in sweats, but now she was decked out in black leggings with a black long-sleeved shirt. Her clothes showed everything and Tevin loved seeing her in them.

Before Tevin could compliment Cassie on how she looked, she spoke up.

"I'm a witch and I know about shifters."

"What?" Tevin practically shouted.

"Witch's magic." Mac whispered with a hint of awe.

Cassie looked up at him with a grin. "Surprise!"

"She handled the shifter just fine. We had a bit of a hiccup afterwards, but got that sorted out too."

"You're The Witch..." Mac's eyes crinkled together at the corner.

"Um, a witch, yes. And you are?"

"I'm Mac, and you're here to fulfill an ancient promise."

"How do you know about that?" Cassie crossed her arms over her chest and her eyes narrowed as she stared at the old shifter.

"The same reason you know about it, I guess. Someone at some point in time wrote it down. We've been waiting for you."

"What?" Both Tevin and Cassie asked at the same time.

"She's the final piece, Tevin."

"What? No, I'm not. I'm here because some idiot in our family promised to help keep some Great Shifter safe a few thousand years ago. But since only griffins and dragons can be Great Shifters, it's an impossible promise to keep."

Vixen's throaty laughter came from behind Tevin. "Does someone want to tell her, or should I?"

Tevin's brain was still processing that Cassie was a witch and supposed to be here, according to Mac, to worry about Vixen and Bray's arrival.

"Tell me what?" Cassie leaned to the side and peered around Tevin.

"Let's all go inside and talk about this." Vixen brushed past everyone and entered the Lodge.

And everyone followed behind her, without any questions. Tevin couldn't feel her using the power all Alphas had to compel him, which meant she was using her voice. She must have been working on it with Mac, since she had trouble controlling it the last time she tried it with the pack.

"I'm Vixen and this is my mate, Bray. There are others, and you'll meet them soon enough, but for now, know that no harm will come to you here."

"I know." Cassie looked over at Tevin and smiled. "Someone already made me that same promise."

He reached for her hand and when she didn't pull away from him, a tiny bit of Tevin's anxiety faded away.

"We're going to have to talk more after this." Tevin leaned down and whispered in her ear.

Cassie bumped her shoulder against his. "I know."

That she didn't argue was a pleasant surprise, but when she squeezed his fingers his wolf howled with pleasure. He would have too if it wouldn't have caused everyone to look at him as though he had gone crazy.

"Tevin?" Mac asked from behind.

"Yeah?"

"About that man you saw. Could you touch him?"

"What do you mean?"

"When you went for him, could you touch him?"

"Oh, yeah, no I couldn't."

"What man?" Cassie asked.

"Later, baby."

As they came to the doorway to the kitchen, Mac cleared his throat. Vixen pivoted and leveled her stare on the old shifter.

He didn't flinch under her glare. He swiped off the worn hat he always had on top of his head and combed his gnarled fingers through his wild gray hair.

"I think this conversation needs to wait. There are things I need to look up and some calls I need to make." Mac turned his attention to Maddie and swung his arm around her shoulder. "I believe you can help me with that last bit, lass."

Maddie and Mac left the group behind and headed toward the front of the Lodge.

"He can be so infuriating sometimes." Vixen planted her hands on her hips and glared at the empty space behind Tevin.

"Tell me about it." Bray frowned and looked over at Tevin.

Vixen's attention swiveled away from Mac's abrupt departure to Cassie. She didn't look away. Instead, Cassie matched Vixen's commanding gaze with a haughty look of her own.

"I suppose it's time we start building those cabins we've been putting off building."

"Already on it." Bray grinned and reached for Vixen's hand. "Come on, Vi, you can look over the orders and make sure I haven't missed anything."

"You aren't as good at distracting me as you think." Vixen said.

She followed along behind Bray, who led her down toward his office. Away from the bedrooms. She even dragged her feet, much the same way Cassie had the night before.

Oh, fuck.

How come he hadn't seen it sooner? Cassie was just like Vixen.

"Come on. Before Vixen changes her mind." Tevin squeezed Cassie's hand and led her down the hallway to his bedroom.

CHAPTER SIXTEEN

TEVIN sat on the edge of his bed watching Cassandra as she stood in the middle of the room. She had started the conversation sitting next to him, but at some point she stood and began pacing. He said he told her everything and wasn't going to do things by halves anymore. Even if what he told her put her in danger.

What he wouldn't explain was the man Mac had asked him about. Or why it was important enough for Mac to put off having a conversation that he seemed excited to have.

She wasn't sure she wanted him to tell her everything any more than she wanted him to only share hints. What she did know was that she wanted to be there. Even though Cassandra told her grandma she wanted to go home, she hadn't really believed it.

Cassandra closed her eyes and took a deep breath. Tevin still didn't know about the baby. She should have told him after Tevin shared everything. About Vixen being a griffin and him being a wolf, the prophecy, and how the women and females of the pack fell into the different roles. He promised her that despite all the dangers that came with Broken Peak, he'd do everything in his power to keep her safe as long as she stayed close to him.

She should have told him he was going to be a father.

Tevin was braver than Cassandra.

And now, she was going choose the coward's path again and use sex to put off sharing her secret.

No. Not sex. They weren't fucking and it wasn't anything like what happened at the bar. This wasn't a one night stand and it wasn't without promises. Tevin promised her more than she'd ever expected. And she returned his gift with a lie by omission.

Cassandra stepped toward him until she stood between his spread legs. Her fingertips dragged across the tops of his thighs. Thick and powerful thighs. Last night, when they shared the bed, she didn't appreciate his body. But now that she planned on using it as a distraction, she wanted to be selfish and use it to fully admire the body hidden beneath his clothes.

His hands fisted and he pressed them into the mattress. Tevin stared up at her without blinking. She gazed down and smiled. He nodded, not needing words to urge her to continue.

She couldn't help from staring into his blue eyes when his pupils dilated with what she hoped was arousal. She bent her head down and he tilted his head back. Before their lips neared, hers parted in anticipation of what she'd been dreaming about for the past month. Her mouth found his and while the kiss was gentle, his mouth was just as demanding as the first time he kissed her.

Her memories skated back to that night at the Dirty Whistle. The night she succumbed to Tevin's magical seduction causing her to throw away all caution. The same thing was happening now, except this time it wasn't about sex. It was about her life as she knew it. Whenever Tevin was around, she wanted to put her life behind her and jump into the world he inhabited. She cared more about him than the life she would be leaving behind.

Cassandra pressed her palm against his cheek and he leaned into her touch, but continued kissing her. When she pulled away and stepped back, his body leaned forward to follow her. But she had other plans.

Tevin watched her, his lips lifting a crooked grin that told her he would allow her to continue until he grew tired of the game. Heat rushed to her belly, reinforcing her desire. The night at the Dirty Whistle wasn't a fluke. Despite the promise of no promises, neither could keep it. This broken promise didn't bring along any disappointment.

Tevin worked his fingers down the buttons of his shirt, but his gaze never drifted from her face. He never stopped looking at her. When the last button was unfastened, he stood up and toed off his boots then padded across the floor on sock-covered feet.

Three steps. That's all it took before Tevin stood in front of Cassandra. His hand found her breast and he brushed his thumb across her nipple. It tightened beneath the fabric and she whimpered. She wanted more.

Reaching down to the hem of her shirt, he lifted it up, and she raised her arms to help. The shirt hit the floor once free of her body and his thumb returned to her nipple, circling the aroused flesh through the thin fabric of the camisole she wore beneath the shirt. Her nipple tightened even more. The pleasure shifting into the ache caused by need.

Her whimpers turned into moans.

She reached out to him, wanting his shirt gone, so she could see and touch his skin, but he took her wrists in his hands and pushed them down to her sides. Cassandra pressed her shoulders back, pushing her body closer to him.

He grinned and looked down at her breasts. Her breasts rose beneath the confines of the camisole as she breathed deeply. Tevin watched their movement and now it was Cassandra's turn to smile.

He released her wrists and his fingers tugged at the bottom of the camisole. It came up over her head as quickly as the shirt. She expected his hand to return to her breast, instead he stepped back and exhaled.

Looking into his eyes, she noticed the flashes of silver behind the blue and the unasked question. Did she want this?

Finding the words to convey what she wanted was an impossible task. Even the smile and small nod could only give a fraction of her wants and desires.

He lowered his gaze, but not before she saw that his eyes had turned completely silver.

The fluttering in her belly moved lower, reacting to the heat in his gaze. She shifted her weight from foot to foot, pressing her thighs together in an attempt to increase the friction and alleviate the need to have him pressed up against her.

Flesh brushed flesh as his thumb found her nipple. She moaned louder. The ignored nipple tightened in a combination of need and sympathy.

Cassandra lowered her eyes, no longer able to control her body's response to the naked lust in his eyes. The sight of his erection beneath his jeans greeted her. She knew he was larger. She had held him in her hands, had him inside her. But having time to themselves gave her the opportunity to appreciate just how large he was.

She gasped and Tevin laughed. Like he read her mind and knew her thoughts.

His hand left her breast and his fingertips pressed against her chin until once more she looked into his eyes. Once satisfied, his hands slid down her body to her hips, and he rolled the waistband of the leggings down. If he noticed that there was a surplus of fabric around the waist, he didn't say anything. Tevin dropped to his knees, but kept his eyes locked on hers.

She stepped free of the leggings and stood before him in only a pair of panties. Tevin lowered his gaze then stood, taking the time to enjoy the sight of her body. When his eyes found hers again, she smiled.

Cassandra ran her tongue across her dry lips, moistening them, and his smile fell as he responded with a groan. Tevin stepped back again and raised his arm towards the bed. She didn't understand what he wanted from her, and sat down on the edge of the bed to wait.

Even with the panties on, she kept her knees together. Not because she was shy, but because of the need growing within her. Tevin laughed again. A sound so soft it might have been an embrace.

He prowled towards the bed. Stalking her as though she was an innocent animal oblivious to the danger of the big bad wolf. His shirt fell to the ground before his fingers worked on the button and zipper of his pants. It wasn't as though he was stripping for her, but the slow uncovering of his body was more erotic than anything she'd seen before.

Standing in front of her, he pressed her shoulders to the bed and covered her body with his naked one.

She pushed up against him, needing to feel him everywhere at once. Careful of not putting too much weight on her, he ran his hands down her arm to her wrist and raised it over her head. He did the same to the other arm and her body stretched out beneath him.

"Can you keep your hands where they are, Cassie?"

The sound of his voice sent a charge through her body.

She struggled with what he asked of her. She wanted to touch him and run her hands all over his body, but he didn't want that. And he wasn't really asking her if she could keep her hands in place, Tevin wanted to know if she would do as he asked. She nodded, unable to find the words.

His fingertips skated along her arms, dragging lightly across her skin. He avoided her breasts even though she arched her back, hoping to guide his touch. His forefinger circled her navel, moving outward in a slow spiral. Cassandra's stomach fluttered under his maddening touch.

She wanted more, but wasn't sure how to ask for it. Tevin dragged his fingers over her hips, hooking the waist of her panties and pulling them down her thighs then off. His hands returned to her thighs, parting her legs for him.

As he slid up her body, she hoped he would stop and pay attention to so many different places. But he continued until his mouth found hers. When his tongue brushed her lips, her mouth opened for him.

Before she realized it, her arms wrapped around his neck, and she pulled him closer.

Tevin stopped and sat up over her. He gently placed her arms back where he had placed them. When he looked down at her, she returned his gaze and moistened her lips again, ready to speak. But before any words could escape, Tevin pressed his finger against her lips and shook his head.

No words. He wanted silence.

His gaze locked on her eyes. She couldn't look away from him, even if she had wanted to. Finally, after several seconds, she nodded. If he didn't want her to use words, then she would have to use other ways to communicate.

He bent down and whispered in her ear, sending a shudder through her body.

"Good girl."

His hands returned to the exploration of her body. Thankfully, this time, he didn't avoid her breasts. His palms cupped them as he ran his thumb across her nipples. She lifted up towards him and her head fell back against the bed. His lips discovered her newly exposed neck and his tongue ran from her collarbone up to her jaw then back to her collarbone before moving down. When his tongue found her nipple, he wrapped his lips around it.

The tip of his tongue flicked against the tight bud and she moaned. With care, he bit down gently and only released it from his teeth when her breath caught as pleasure shifted in the realm of discomfort. Tevin looked up at her and smirked, but kissed the now tender nipple. He kissed his way down her stomach and along her hips.

The male was brilliant at avoiding the areas she wanted him to focus on.

Tevin lifted his chin and gazed at her face, and she bent her head to look down at him. Her hips lifted, anticipating his next move. He watched her as his lips brushed over her skin until his mouth hovered just over her clit.

Cassandra wanted to beg, scream, and plead for him to hurry up. But Tevin didn't want words. The need to give him what he wanted overruled her own needs. He pursed his lips and blew. A reward for obeying and remaining silent.

Her hips shot off the bed and his tongue flicked over the tip of her clit the same way it had over her nipple. She might have been able to control her voice, but she lost control of her body. Her hips bucked up again and he growled. The noise vibrated against her legs, and she willed herself to keep her arms in place.

So maddening, and yet she couldn't help but notice the heightened state of her arousal. He slowly built it up until it was the only thing she could focus on.

He lowered his mouth, holding her hips in place as his tongue explored her pussy. If he hadn't held her, she would have writhed beneath him. When his tongue entered her, she gave up what little control she had. Her fists pounded the mattress and her body bucked against his. As wonderful as his tongue felt, she needed more from him.

Tevin's lips returned to her clit, and he slowly slid a finger inside her. When he added a second finger then moved them slowly in and out while sucking her clit, she grabbed the comforter to keep herself from writhing off the bed. She mourned the lost time with him and his talented mouth.

A warmth grew inside of her, threatening to escape. Her muscles tightened around his fingers. Tevin's teeth, tongue, and lips assaulted her clit. He rested his arm across her stomach, holding her in place.

The release was unstoppable.

She moaned out as the orgasm rolled through her.

Tevin pulled away from her as soon as her body relaxed. He stretched over her body, positioning himself between her legs. A fingertip dragged between her breasts down to her heated arousal. His touch settled the aftershocks as she caught her breath and looked up at him.

She'd never believed that everything could be revealed in a look. All the wants, desires, and feelings. But the way Tevin looked down at Cassandra, she believed in all of it.

He bent down and kissed her. She tasted herself on his lips, but didn't hesitate to return the kiss. He growled into her mouth and her body trembled.

His mouth found her ear and he whispered, "good girl."

Those words shouldn't have excited her. Just two small words. But the way he said them and why he said them drove her arousal to even higher levels.

His hands moved to her wrists and he lifted her arms. She wrapped her arms around his shoulder and held her body tight against his. She knew what would happen next, she also understood that feeling him deep inside her would be enough to satisfy her needs. Cassandra didn't want anything separating them.

The head of his cock pressed against her entrance.

They stopped kissing and looked into each other's eyes while he pushed into her. He moved too slowly, taking his time, and she was growing impatient. She didn't know what he wanted, but she knew what she wanted. Her legs wrapped around his waist and pulled him down.

It was enough.

Tevin didn't hold back. He drove into her with a hard thrust. Once his cock was sheathed inside her, he held still.

She couldn't stand the wait. "Please."

"Please what, Cassie?"

"Don't stop. More. Anything. Just please."

He laughed and pressed his lips to hers. Moving slowly at first, he rocked his hips back and forth until her movements matched his. She wanted the hard thrusts from their first night together. She needed to feel his cock entering over and over. Instead, he stayed inside her and rocked his hips, rubbing against the spot guaranteed to rock any woman's world.

Cassandra dragged her hands over his back and stared into his eyes.

They weren't having sex. They weren't fucking. Tevin was making love to her.

Their bodies moved together until she knew she couldn't last, but Tevin wasn't showing any signs of increasing the pace. Just when she figured he had the stamina of a marathon runner, he flipped them over, so he was on his back and she straddled him.

His cock slid deeper into her with the assistance of gravity. She gasped at the intense feeling of fullness, but didn't pull away. He found her clit and pressed his thumb against it.

The muscles in her lower stomach rippled as she tightened around his cock. Tevin didn't move his gaze from hers. She leaned back and placed her hands on his thighs, but didn't look away. Cassandra wasn't willing to lose the sight of his eyes any more than she was willing to release his cock from inside her.

The orgasm built slowly, growing with the combination of their movements and the heat of his stare. From the way the muscles in his stomach tightened, becoming even more defined, she knew he was close too.

"Come with me, Tevin."

He nodded and pressed down hard on her clit while drawing tight circles over it.

So close. She could taste it.

Tevin grabbed her hips, digging his fingers into the flesh of her ass while thrusting up hard and pulling her down with the same brutal force.

Whatever happened, worked. Her orgasm ripped through her and Tevin followed with an explosion soon after. His hands slid up along her back before wrapping his arms around her. He pulled her down towards him, and she collapsed on top of his body.

Tevin delivered a hard kiss with a hint of tenderness.

When she moved, his arms tightened, keeping her where she was. Cassandra understood his need. She didn't want to be apart either. Stretching out on top of him, she drew random shapes over his chest. Tevin petted her hair and stroked her back. Eventually, both their breathing slowed and their racing hearts relaxed.

With his arms still around her, he shifted them until they stretched out across the bed on their sides facing one another. As he slipped out of her, he rolled off the bed and headed for the closet. When he returned to her with a towel in hand, he carefully cleaned her up before cleaning himself.

Neither one said anything. Not when he pulled the blanket up over her and climbed into bed with her. Not when his body wrapped around hers. And not when his lips pressed against the back of her neck.

After several minutes of silence, just as Cassandra was close to falling asleep, Tevin's voice broke the silence.

"How come it feels like we still have more to talk about, Cassie?"

She turned and burrowed against his chest, hiding her face in his warmth. When his fingers brushed her cheek and lifted her face until she looked up at him, Cassandra closed her eyes.

"It can wait, Cassie. We don't need to talk if you don't want to."

She opened her eyes and hoped he couldn't see the guilt pricking at her conscience.

"Today was big. You need to get some rest." His arms tightened around her and pulled her close.

CHAPTER SEVENTEEN

TEVIN lurked in the shadows of the entrance to the front room and watched Cassie and Finley on the couch. Maddie had come to check up on Cassie and told him, in no uncertain terms, that he wasn't a participant, but that he needed to go find her. And now he was creeping around the Lodge watching one of his best friends with his girl.

Shit. His girl? Yeah, he might have known she was his, but he hadn't actually admitted it.

Until now.

What the fuck was wrong with him?

Cassie turned his world inside out and upside down and didn't even know she was doing it.

Jealousy shot through his stomach and pierced his heart. Finley had a mate and wouldn't try anything with Cassie. Tevin knew that. Or at least he thought he knew that. Finley was more like an older brother or close friend. She was closer with Finley than the others. And when they hung out it was like they were planning something that was bound to get them both into trouble.

They sat close to each other with their heads together and looking at something on Finley's phone. Tevin wanted to be in Finley's place. He wanted to be the one sitting with her and sharing whatever it was they were looking at.

Not that she didn't share things with Tevin though. In the past few days she'd taught him about magic and witches, and he taught her about shifters and wolves. He just didn't enjoy watching Finley doing what *he* wanted to be doing with Cassie.

Tevin cleared his throat and stepped into the room. "What are you looking at?"

"No fucking clue, but I can't stop watching. It's like a train wreck and a UFO landing all at once."

Cassie didn't look up from the screen. "We found the part of the internet that shouldn't exist, but would be incomplete without it."

"Porn?" Tevin asked as he moved closer. He wanted her to invite him to join them, but didn't want to stay in the shadows.

"So much better." Finley grinned. "This is some seriously fucked up shit."

Tevin couldn't wait for the invitation. He closed the distance between them, but Finley's and Cassie's heads hid the screen. He held his hand out and Finley set the phone on his palm without an argument. He looked down at the screen.

What. The. Ever. Loving. Fuck.

He-Man was singing along with the song *What's Up* by 4 Non Blondes. Or at least that's what he thought he was looking at.

He dropped the phone back into Finley's hand. "That's fucking weird, Fin."

"I know, but I can't stop watching it. And that's the only song he sings too. I just can't turn away from it." He pointed a finger and laughed at Cassie. "And it's her fault too. We were looking at random sites and next thing I know, we've been sitting here for over thirty minutes watching the same two-minute clip over and over. I am officially in the part of the internet that I'd be better off knowing never existed."

"Maddie's here, Cassie. She's waiting in the bedroom for you." Tevin headed down to the kitchen and expected them to follow.

Sure enough, both Finley and Cassie hurried down the hallway right behind him. Cassie turned off to head to their bedroom and Finley followed Tevin into the kitchen.

Shit. He should have taken Cassie to the bedroom. Instead of being the good male he wanted to be for her, he walked away.

But he needed to keep his distance. At least that's what he told himself. Yeah, he wanted her to stay with him. And, yeah, his wolf had practically claimed her. But eventually she'd want to leave. Even if Mac was convinced she was The Witch, Cassie would walk away from him. Someday she'd get tired of the danger that came part and parcel with Broken Peak, and he'd be left alone again. Back where he was after their first night together at the Dirty Whistle almost six weeks ago.

"Eleanor wants to interview Cassandra. She's been bugging me to talk with you about it."

"Tell her it can wait. You get her checked out of the hotel?"

"Yep, and even grabbed her car. It's in the garage along with the others. Sweet little ride too."

"Good." Tevin made a note to talk with Danielle and figure out what else they needed to do to erase Cassie's footprint in War.

That hyena had been here for her, everyone was certain about that. And the man who only Tevin could see had mentioned a witch.

"There's also the discussion she needs to have with Mac. Whatever Maddie said will only hold them off for so long. Mac and Vixen are going to corner her eventually and start asking questions." Finley added another complication to Tevin's life.

"Well, she's sick, right? Plus, there's also what happened with the hyena shifter. It should buy her some more time."

"Whatever. Just letting you know that once they get a whiff of something they're like a dog with a bone and won't let up until they get what they want from it." Finley shrugged. "Speaking of dogs, Moose is a little fucker, isn't he?"

"Yeah, I caught him staring down Foster's wolf the other day. It's like the dog doesn't have an ounce of sense."

"Don't you think it's kind of strange how he fits in with us?"

"What do you mean?" Tevin grabbed a bottle of water from the fridge.

"He won't back down from Bray. I mean, he keeps away from Vixen, but that's understandable. It's almost like he's part of our pack. Like if we went for a run, he'd be right there with us."

"He's driving my wolf crazy. Marking every tree and bush he can find. But Cassie loves him."

"Kinda like Danielle and her hamster." Tevin snickered. "Except we don't have to worry about Foster eating Moose."

"Naw, it's something more."

"You think maybe, since Cassandra's a witch, that her dog isn't what it seems?"

"What? No. Moose is definitely a dog. You can smell him."

"Yeah, but don't witches have familiars?" Finley asked.

"Those are cats, moron."

"Just saying, he's a weird ass dog."

He was also growing on Tevin. Every morning he woke up and let Moose outside, gave him some breakfast, and then let him back inside, so he could cuddle with Cassie in bed before she woke up. As much as Moose kept an eye on Cassie, he also liked to follow Tevin around. And Tevin's wolf was as curious about Moose as Moose was about Tevin.

But before Moose met Tevin's Wolf, he wanted Cassie to meet him. After that first night's discussion neither of them really spoke about the shifter or magic thing.

Maybe it was time to stop putting off the discussion with Mac and Vixen.

Maddie cleared her throat from the kitchen doorway, interrupting Tevin's thoughts. "Finley. You mind?"

"Nope. Not at all." Finley hurried from the kitchen. "Pocket should be done with whatever she was doing with Vixen.

Maddie sat down at the table and gestured to the chair across from her.

"Is Cassie alright?" Tevin slowly sat down. In his experience, when someone told you to sit, bad news followed.

"She's fine."

"So you're saying we can't keep Vixen and Mac from interrogating her anymore?"

Maddie shifted in her seat. It was like she had something she wanted to tell him, but just when he thought she would open up, Cassie usually interrupted. Which wasn't a bad interruption at all. She was getting bored and when the boredom got too much, she usually found him and dragged him to the bedroom.

But she'd spent almost an entire week inside now. The only time she went outside was to sit on the porch.

Tevin needed to come up with a reason why Cassie needed to stay at Broken Peak and not go back to the hotel. But that wasn't nearly as important as figuring out why Maddie was being so cagey.

He stared across the table at Maddie, using the glare Bray used on them when the Alpha knew they fucked up and wanted them to confess.

Maddie returned the stare. Didn't even try to look away.

Shit, she wouldn't cave easily, but Tevin knew she was hiding something and had been hiding something since he saw her talking to Vixen.

Tevin opened the bottle of water and took a long drink before setting it down on the table. "I can trust you, Maddie?"

"I would hope so. We've done how many patrols together?"

"So why does it feel like you're hiding something big from me? Something I don't think you want to be hiding, but can't or won't share?"

Maddie said nothing. Just blinked slowly at Tevin.

He rested his forearms on the edge of the table and didn't look away. "What were you meeting with Vixen about?"

"I told you I had to swing by Mac's, and she happened to be there."

"Vixen doesn't do chatting, Maddie. Stop lying." Tevin went in for the kill. He'd seen the females use guilt with their mates enough times to have a handle on the skill. "I consider you a close friend, Maddie. But friends don't lie to each other."

Maddie's eyes went hard.

Oh, shit.

Maybe he didn't have a handle on the guilt skill.

Yeah, Tevin dealt a low blow, they both knew it.

"I haven't ever lied, Tev. Never. But, there are some things that I can't always share. If you don't trust me anymore, fine." Maddie stood and pushed away from the table. "Tell Cassandra I said bye. I don't want her to think I'm rude or don't like her."

Shit.

Maddie stalked out of the kitchen and up the hall to the front room. She even slammed the door behind her. Tevin fucked up. Maddie was pissed. Really pissed.

She'd cool down eventually, or at least he hoped she would. Then he could fix things. Maddie was one of the few friends Cassie liked, and she'd be hurt if Maddie stayed away because of him.

Cassie tolerated the others, but she talked with Maddie and Finley. Hell, he'd even considered asking Vixen if Maddie could move in temporarily. There was a good chance Cassie would be as pissed as Maddie.

Without realizing it, Tevin headed toward their bedroom. He knocked on the door and expected Cassie to open it right away, but instead he could hear things being moved around.

The sounds bothered the fuck out him. If she just had a stomach bug, then how come Maddie had to bring in all that equipment. He knocked on the door again then tried the knob. It was locked.

What the fuck?

First Maddie and whatever secret she was hiding and now Cassie.

"Open the fucking door, Cassie."

Cassie's voice came from behind the door, but it was muffled and Tevin couldn't make out any words. He was going to break the fucking door down if he had to.

The door opened before it came to the breaking it down part and Cassie's head popped through the crack. "Give me a few, okay?"

She shut the door, but Tevin stuck his foot in the opening, stopping her.

"Tevin, I'll be out in a few, okay?"

He didn't budge.

She sighed. "Please?"

Cassie looked at him with her beautiful eyes, begging him and he couldn't resist her. Not that he ever could resist her, but using her eyes as an excuse soothed his bruised ego.

"Fine, but will you give me a full report? I want to know if there's something I need to be concerned about. Maybe we need to go see a specialist or something."

"Tev, please." The pleading in her whisper was worse than a kick to the chest.

He stepped away from the door until his back hit the wall, and she closed the door.

What the fuck just happened?

His wolf wondered the same thing.

Tevin couldn't look away from the closed door. He needed to walk away, take a break. But with Maddie gone and Finley busy with his mate, he didn't have anyone to keep her company. And there was no fucking way he was going to leave her alone. Not after she faced down a hyena shifter. Yeah, she might have done fine on her own, but he wouldn't risk leaving her.

He slid down the wall to the floor, crossed his arms over his knees, and buried his head in his arms.

Tevin didn't lose control. Sure, he fought with his packmates, but he'd never lost his cool. But Cassie had witnessed his meltdown.

He wasn't sure how long he'd been sitting on the floor when the door finally opened. Her fingers combed through his hair, brushing it off his face, and he looked up.

Cassie knelt in front of him and pressed her hands against his cheek. Like Foster did whenever he wanted someone's undivided attention.

She wasn't angry.

She should have been. Hell, he was pissed at himself.

"Let's get you a drink and some food."

Tevin blinked up at her, not trusting what he saw. She reached down and took his hand. And he let her. Not because he expected her to help him up, he just wanted to hold her. And keep holding her.

They pushed off the floor and walked in silence to the kitchen. She quietly went about making him a cup of coffee, even adding the dash of cinnamon he secretly liked in his coffee, but never let anyone see him adding.

He studied Cassie as she moved around the kitchen. It was like she belonged here. Which she fucking did if he and his wolf had any say in the matter.

Once the cup of coffee was in front of him, she got herself a bottle of water and sat down across from him. She twisted the cap on and off, avoiding his eyes.

"I want to see my grandma."

Finley tried to warn him something like this would happen.

He took a breath and sipped the coffee, breathing in the scent of cinnamon floating on the surface. "Cassie."

"Tevin, I'm not saying I am going to leave. Just that I want to see my grandma. I get that there are dangers out there, but I was fine in War for a month. Seeing her in town should be safe." She tightened the cap on the bottle and her knuckles turned white. "Besides, the hyena is dead. It's not like he can come after me again. And there haven't been more strange shifters showing up."

How the hell did she know that? He doubted Finley told her and it wasn't like she actually talked to anyone else in the pack. That left Maddie.

Fuck him.

That was her big secret. Maddie shared pack information with Cassie.

"Yeah, but we don't know if someone hired him. We aren't sure what's going on in the shifter world right now, Cassie, or why someone would come after you."

"I can handle myself." She stared at her hands wrapped around the bottle.

He wanted to lift her head so he could see her eyes. He wanted to stare at her, memorize the small details and beautiful elegance of each part that combined to create the most gorgeous female he'd ever seen. There were so many things he wanted. Too many. And if he touched her, it would lead to the conversation being delayed for at least an hour.

Not that he cared. He enjoyed any time he spent with her in the privacy of the bedroom.

He pushed down the urge to give into her and prepared for her anger. Cassie might have not have been angry with his outburst, but she never accepted it without a fight.

Then she looked at him with her big eyes and pushed her hair behind her ear.

Fuck him. He was going to give into her.

"Okay. But we need to meet her in town at a restaurant or something." He set the coffee down and waited for her response. Yeah, he gave into her, but no fucking way was she going off on her own.

"Fine."

Shit. Was that a good fine or a bad fine? He hadn't figured out the fine signs yet.

Cassie opened the bottle and took a long drink. All worries about the meaning of the word fine disappeared. In their place was the image of her lips wrapped around his cock just as tightly as they were around the bottle.

Tevin coughed and shifted in the chair. "We'll get a phone from Danielle and you can call her."

Maybe letting her visit town and see her grandma would be good and settle some of her growing boredom. Or maybe it would all go to shit.

Cassie bounced out of her chair and walked by him with a huge smile. Suddenly it didn't matter if Tevin fucked things up. He made her happy. Well, at least happier than she had been.

Tevin was almost certain he'd been played. But he didn't care. He leaned back in the chair and drank his coffee. As long as she was happy, Cassie could play him as much as she wanted.

CHAPTER EIGHTEEN

TEVIN wove around the racks of clothes. He wouldn't let Cassandra get more than a few feet away. Not even for a minute. She didn't care though. She was finally out. Even if it was only for the afternoon and even if Maggie tagged along. Finley's mate talked a mile a minute, but at least she was entertaining. Memaw even liked her.

She pushed through the racks of clothes, trying to find things she could wear in a few months that didn't shout, *look away from the bump I am hiding!* The last store didn't have anything and this one wasn't much better. Maggie didn't help either. If it sparkled, she held it up and insisted Cassandra would look beautiful in it. To add to the problem, Maggie would show it to Tevin, who gave a nod to everything.

Maggie stepped closer to Cassandra. "We saw you at the Dirty Whistle. I was supposed to dance that night, but we had a change of plans."

Cassandra blushed. They'd all seen her at the bar. Tevin must have said something before heading over to her. That meant the entire pack knew about their one night stand. Great.

"Well maybe we can find another time to go dancing."

"I'd like that." Maggie's head bobbed up and down.

Memaw rolled her eyes at the tiny female, and showed Cassandra a loose fitting tunic. The way her grandma smiled at her, Cassandra knew that she saw the way Tevin looked at her. However, things began, he was hers. The idea settled in Cassandra's thoughts like a warm blanket.

"Come on, let's try on some clothes." Memaw pushed Maggie to the dressing room, whose arms were overflowing with everything she'd picked up.

Tevin stomped his way behind them, but when they got to the doorway to the dressing rooms, Memaw stopped him. "You can stay out here."

Tevin ignored Memaw and looked at Cassandra. She grinned and shrugged. What could she do? Her grandma was a force of nature.

Cassandra entered an empty dressing room and Memaw handed her a stack of hangers with clothes. "Next stop is a shoe store. Those boots aren't great with leggings."

She didn't tell her grandma that after giving up on making her pants fasten on their own, she was down to three choices. Find an elastic to extend the button, wear a pencil skirt, or wear a pair of leggings. Cassandra hung the clothes on the hooks and grinned at her grandma's choices. Nothing had a fitted waist.

Cassandra tried on the first shirt and stepped out for Memaw's approval. If she agreed then Cassandra let Tevin offer his opinion. Maggie pretty much loved everything, which was great for her ego, but not a good barometer for how good it actually looked on her.

She discovered that Tevin's eyes would light up if she twirled for him. And since he hadn't been grumpy or complained once, she didn't mind twirling if it made him happy.

Tevin stood at the counter with an arm around her waist, holding her tight against his body. She didn't understand it. It wasn't like Cassandra would run away at the first opportunity. But she didn't mind him holding her either and pressed closer. He handed the clerk cash for their purchases and Memaw pursed her lips in that knowing way of hers.

Memaw approved of Tevin. From what Cassandra had learned, packs, especially smaller packs, ran things more as a family. Meaning the pack bought everyone their clothes, not just Tevin. But Memaw didn't have to know that.

One hour, four bags, which Tevin carried, and a still chattering Maggie later, they left the store and headed to the shoe store Maggie found on her phone. Maggie barreled right to the display table in the middle of the store. She picked up the different shoes with multiple oohs and ahhs.

"I've got it." Memaw hurried after Maggie before they had a small catastrophe on their hands.

"Shoes?" Tevin asked while reaching for her hand after he shifted all the bags to one hand.

"For some people, not me, but it's possible for Maggie, shoes are more addictive than heroin.

"Finley will kill both of us." Tevin pulled her closer.

"I'll find another website for him to get lost in." She couldn't help but smile at the sight of his gorgeous face.

Cassandra blamed the poppy seed for always wanting to race off to the nearest bed with Tevin. Except that wasn't fair to the poppy seed considering it wasn't present that night at the bar. Well, not until after.

It was the way Tevin looked at her. His full lips and dark hair. And his blue eyes that flashed silver. She'd deny it if anyone asked, but it was also his bossiness. He expected things and part of her enjoyed that. Since he absconded with her from The Old Jail, everything Tevin did, had been what he thought was best for her. Yeah, it pissed her off half the time, but he didn't make his decisions based on his wants. He made them based on her needs.

He didn't keep her locked away because he didn't trust her. Tevin kept her at Broken Peak because he believed she wasn't safe on her own. After the episode with the hyena, maybe she wasn't.

Cassandra looked over at Tevin, watching him the way he watched her. She couldn't help herself. Pushing up on her toes, she brushed her lips against his. She might not always agree with him, but she never doubted his motivations.

"What was that for?" He asked with a smile. "Not that I'm complaining."

"Does there have to be a reason?"

Tevin bent his head forward, lowering his mouth to her ear. Instead of whispering something naughty, like she secretly hoped he would, he kissed the small patch of skin below her ear.

"Okay, kissing time is over." Memaw came up behind them, interrupting the sweet moment. "I can only keep Maggie distracted for so long, and she's just discovered platform heels. She can't walk on them, but she's convinced they can be used as weapons. People are starting to stare."

They should have brought the others with them. But in fairness, Maggie sort of invited herself along. And Cassandra didn't want Finley to get upset because she hurt Maggie's feelings, so she'd agreed.

Memaw pulled Cassandra away from Tevin, and he let her go, but not before squeezing her hand.

"And don't think we won't be having a little talk later, young man." Memaw added before they reached Maggie standing at the display of shoes that had to have been from a line designed for stripper assassins. Maggie hadn't been wrong. The shoes would make great weapons.

Somehow, they managed to spend more time at the shoe store than the clothing store. Even better, Tevin didn't insist on standing less than a foot away from her while she looked over the shoes like he had at the clothing store. Except Cassandra didn't know if the change pleased her or disappointed her.

"I know that look, Cassandra. What are you thinking so hard about?" Memaw whispered, so they wouldn't distract Maggie and garner more stares.

"I didn't know I was."

"Cassandra, your best and worst quality is that you can't play poker to save your life. You might as well have steam coming out of your ears for how much your mind is churning away at something." Memaw sat down in a chair and leaned back, stretching out her legs. "When I first met your grandfather he was overbearing and overprotective, nothing compared to Tevin, but I think we both know what that is. But I digress. My point is that most women would kill for a man to look at them the way Tevin looks at you.

She pulled on a pair of ballet flats and looked up at her grandma. "How does he look at me?

"Like you're the only woman on the planet. That woman at the other store practically threw herself on him and he ignored her. Your grandfather looked at me that way. Not so much your father with your mother. And you know how that ended."

Cassandra knew exactly how it ended. Her mother and father divorced before she turned five and then her mom left Cassandra with her grandma so she could explore the world. Her mom wasn't a bad mom, just not a present mom. Cassandra didn't doubt her mother's love, but she did doubt her father even remembered her name, much less her birthday.

"He ignored her?" Cassandra wiggled her toes in the shoes and stood to test how it felt to walk around in them.

"You are not a dumb woman, Cassandra. Don't pretend that you are. You aren't good at it." Memaw winked at her. "One thing I can't figure out. There's no mention of him in The Book. Get that pair, they'll be comfortable and will stretch."

Memaw patted her knee and leaned back in her chair with a self-satisfied smile.

"When do you have to go back?"

"Hm? Oh, I don't know. Whenever."

Cassandra narrowed her eyes at Memaw's evasive answer. Her grandma was up to something, but she had no idea what. "Well, while today was fun and all, I thought maybe we could talk. Just the two of us?"

She needed to speak with her grandma about the baby. It was one thing for a witch to be born into a family of witches and a shifter to be born in a pack of shifters. But a baby that was both shifter and witch? That was an unknown and presented a pile of problems the size of Mt. Everest.

"That would be nice, but that might require you finding a distraction for Tevin."

Her grandma wasn't wrong. There was no way Tevin would let her out of his sight, much less be alone. "I can call you."

She might be able to convince Tevin a simple phone call was safe enough. And if protested, she'd just drag him back to the bedroom. Not that it was a chore. Tevin was amazing in the bedroom.

"You're getting that look again." Memaw shook her head in exasperation. "Cassandra, as long as he's good to you, I'm happy. But be careful."

Memaw glanced at Cassandra's stomach before looking over at Maggie and her growing stockpile of stripper shoes.

Her grandma didn't need to say anything else. Cassandra understood. The situation was already complicated. If it wasn't for whatever was in The Book, Memaw would have dragged Cassandra back to their happy little farmhouse.

Cassandra looked for Tevin, holding up the pair of shoes she'd tired on. When she found him, his gaze was locked on her.

"Don't worry, Memaw, Tevin won't let me be anything but careful."

CHAPTER NINETEEN

STACKS of books, some opened and some closed, along with piles of paper, and an army of notebooks covered the surface of the mammoth table in the kitchen.

Eleanor and Mac brought everything they had out and now Vixen, Bray, Eleanor, Mac, Cassie, Tevin, and even Maddie were pouring over the pages.

"This makes no fucking sense." Tevin grumbled at the words on the page.

"Maybe you should have paid more attention when Mac and I talked about this." Eleanor flipped the page of the journal she was reading, not bothering to look up.

"But we're not looking at the mumbo jumbo, and yes, I did pay attention. It was impossible not to for how much you all fucking talk about it."

Cassie looked over at him and grinned, which was enough for him to return to his task.

Mac had sat Tevin down with Vixen and Bray and made him explain exactly what he saw after Cassie had done her magic blast. At first, he had been worried about anyone believing him about seeing the man since no one could sense him, but his Alphas had taken the news as a matter of fact.

It also helped that Mac thought there might be a new player on the board and was making himself, or themselves, known.

For the past two hours, they'd poured over every book and journal, looking for any mention of something similar to Tevin's experience. So far, they'd found nothing.

"In med school, we're taught that if we hear hoof beats, not to assume it's a zebra." Maddie looked up from the paper she'd been examining and looked at Tevin.

Their relationship wasn't back to where it was before the blow up, but they were better. She was talking with him at least. He let her know that he wasn't angry about her sharing that there hadn't been any more strange shifters in the territory, and she'd been okay with his half-assed apology. Besides, it wasn't like Cassie and Maddie could spend any time together if Maddie was still pissed at him. Although Tevin didn't believe Maddie had a reason for being upset, he wasn't going to focus on that particular detail.

"What's that supposed to mean?" Tevin asked.

"We're not assuming it's a zebra and maybe we should." Maddie raised her hand palm out, stopping both Vixen's and Eleanor's protests before they even came out. "None of us, including a witch, can explain what happened. And we have several types of shifters here too. One who shouldn't exist. At least not that any of us knew about."

"We do have access to another." Cassie looked across the table at Maddie. "It wouldn't hurt to ask him."

"Who?" Eleanor asked, ever the curious one.

"No." Mac shook his head. "He's already too involved for my liking."

"All right, not him, but we do have someone else who might be able to help." Vixen declared while looking at Cassie.

While everyone else was busy trying to figure out who Maddie and Cassie were talking about, and who Mac and Vixen also apparently knew, Tevin worried about having to face Sybil Voisin once again. The old lady was nice enough, in a slightly eccentric way, but she was also Cassie's grandma and that messed with both Tevin and Tevin's wolf. If Sybil didn't approve of Tevin, Cassie would walk away from him.

"I can call her," Cassie said. "Put her on speaker phone?"

Mac studied the accumulation of knowledge on the table. "No. A call isn't going to help. She needs to be here."

Great. Just what Tevin needed. Sybil learning that he was crazy and experienced hallucinations and dragging Cassie away faster than he could blink.

Vixen handed Cassie a phone. "Call her. We can send Jackson to pick her up."

Someone knocked on the front door before Cassie even picked up the phone.

Six heads turned to the kitchen doorway. No one knocked. Ever. Even if someone wasn't part of the pack, they just walked in. Most guests who just showed up were all expected. And those who weren't expected weren't guests and the pack and its allies took care of them as soon as the alarms went off.

"Hello!"

What th-

"Memaw!"

"No need for niceties, I'll just follow the sounds to find you all."

Cassie jumped to her feet and practically tripped getting away from the table to greet her grandma.

"The Book decided it wanted to cooperate now." Sybil stepped into the kitchen, gave a cursory glance to everyone in the room, then threw one of the biggest books Tevin had ever seen onto the table. "Apparently, it's done being petulant."

Mac pushed away from the table and stood, combing his fingers through his wild hair in what might have been an attempt to tame it. "Sybil."

"Mac." The older woman nodded to Mac. "Well, are you going to introduce me?"

"You two know each other?" Cassie shot her grandma an accusing glare.

"In a way." Mac answered. "Sybil Voisin, this is Bray and Vixen, the Alphas of Broken Peak Pack. Maddie here is a friend. And you already know Tevin. And Eleanor is our resident researcher and also a member of the pack."

Sybil stared at Eleanor as she sat at the table, as though she belonged there. "The Historian."

"What?" Everyone asked at once.

"You come from a long and broad line who is probably more responsible for this," Sybil waved her hand over the books on the table, "than anyone else."

"What? I was just a PhD candidate." Eleanor brushed the comment aside.

"And so were many of the others. Trust me, without your ancestors' help, none of us would be sitting here right now." Sybil looked over at Mac. "And the others?"

"They're around. But they wouldn't be much help at the moment, so Vixen sent them off."

"The Book isn't completely done with its mood. I knew to come here, but not why." Sybil reached for her book and pulled it in front of her.

Cassie sat back down in her chair, but hadn't stopped glaring at her grandma. Tevin reached over and ran his hand over her thigh. Somehow, he just knew her bad mood towards her grandma would come back and bite him. If he could just get her calmed down a small bit, she might not be as angry with him.

"Tell her, Tevin."

Well, there went his plans for staying out of it all. He took a deep breath and retold the story about seeing a man who wasn't there and knew about Cassie being a witch, even before Tevin found out.

After Tevin finished, Sybil shook her head slowly. "I've never heard of anyone projecting themselves like that before. Earth magic doesn't work that way, so it couldn't have been a witch. But that doesn't mean we can't figure it out. The Book wanted me here for some reason, so let's see what it can tell us."

"What is that book?" Eleanor asked while leaning across the table to get a closer look at it.

"The history of the Voisins. Just like you have the MacAllister histories, and I'm sure other shifters have their own histories too. Only a handful of the histories cross though. And the ones that do aren't really complete."

"What do you mean?" Eleanor asked.

"For the most part the histories stay locked within their own little bubble. Most of ours just covers what our ancestors did and what might be expected of their descendants." Cassie filled in the details for Eleanor while her grandma flipped through the pages. "The few times it crosses, as Memaw calls it, are when we have a direct contact. Like the promise someone made thousands of years ago on what turned out to be on my behalf."

"No, it was made on behalf of the Voisin name. Fate just intervened and decided you were the one to fulfill it." Sybil corrected her.

Tevin stared at Cassie. She'd never told him exactly why she was in War. They'd all assumed she was tied in someway to the assignment Vixen gave him.

"So you came here because a book told you to?" Tevin asked her.

"Sort of. There were some other details, like Memaw locking me out of the house, that helped me decide. And I didn't plan on staying."

"But you did stay." Sybil murmured knowingly while she continued flipping pages.

"Yeah, but that wasn't by choice."

"It wasn't?" Tevin asked.

"Not really. Let's just say I had help in keeping me from leaving."

"Who?" Vixen jumped in.

Maddie leaned back in her chair. "The one none of you want to ask for help."

Tevin had never felt so lost in his life. The flood of new information overwhelmed what he thought he knew.

Eleanor sat back with a sigh. "I am so lost and I've spent months looking through these journals. Does anyone want to fill me in? And don't you think it would have been helpful to know all this before you gave us this task, Mac?"

Mac ignored Eleanor's question and instead stared at Vixen, who stared right back at him, but neither said a word.

Cassie slid her chair closer to Tevin as the silence weighed down on everyone. Whatever was going on didn't seem to have a resolution in the near future and Tevin didn't like it. He wrapped his arm around her shoulders.

"For crying out loud." Sybil slammed her hands down on the table breaking the stalemate. "This isn't just about you all, and it's high time you recognized that. Yeah, you're big players, but there's a bigger player and sometimes his interests don't align with yours. Trust me when I say we've all been there. But as far as I know, he's never done anything that I would consider harmful."

"I just don't trust him." Mac grumbled.

"Who?" Tevin snapped. He was done with not knowing.

"Alexander." Maddie answered.

If Tevin thought learning who everyone was talking about would have cleared things up, he was mistaken. If anything he was more lost. "Who's Alexander?"

"He's tied to the prophecies." Bray finally spoke up. Whatever was going on, he had had enough. "It goes back to a war that happened thousands of years ago. Apparently alliances were made."

"And so were bargains, but none of the participants understood what the cost would be," Sybil said

"Still confused." Tevin's patience was growing thin.

"Same here, and I know about this stuff. Or some of it at least." Cassie grumbled and leaned toward Tevin.

"Your histories wouldn't have any of this part since, as far as I know, the shifters didn't participate. Which is also why you probably weren't aware of the different supernaturals."

"Well, we know about some of them. Like the mindwipers." Vixen narrowed her eyes at Sybil, as though she was measuring the old woman as a foe instead of a friend.

"Yes, yes, but they're recent and weren't around for the Concord."

"What concord?" Mac asked.

"The one where all the supernaturals gave their power to one in order to destroy the Great Shifters. At least one witch family didn't join, the Voisins, which is why we are here now. Before the Great Shifters were destroyed, they promised to keep the Voisin line safe as long as a Voisin would keep the Great Shifter safe when they emerged."

Everyone sat back in their seats, digesting the information. Finally, Tevin turned to Cassie. "You knew about shifters and that I was one?"

"Well, yeah. Not what you were, but that you were a shifter. Although, to be fair, I didn't believe there was a Great Shifter."

"But how come I didn't know you were a witch?"

Cassie shrugged. "Probably because I didn't use my magic."

"Did you know?" Tevin looked over Cassie's head at Maddie.

"That she was a witch? No, not until right before you learned."

"What about Alexander? Who is this guy and how do you know him?" The pieces were only just now starting to fall into place, but there were still gaping holes.

"He helped Gareth get the financing for the bar. I'm not sure when he showed up in War exactly, but he's interested in the town."

"He's also the one who let us know that shifters were in town asking around about Delia." Bray added.

"So what is he?" Tevin asked.

"The one who received all the power and destroyed the Great Shifters." Sybil spoke with a hushed tone, letting her words settle in everyone's mind.

CHAPTER TWENTY

IT WAS bad enough when they spent hours looking through books that didn't have any answers, but the past hour had been worse. Sybil and Mac had argued about whether they needed to ask Alexander for help.

"We need to keep him out of this." Mac repeated the same argument he'd used twenty times before.

"We can't."

"Yes we can."

They were worse than children bickering. After twenty minutes, Vixen and Bray left, figuring one of them would come and find them once the argument ended. Eleanor gave up thirty minutes into it, making an excuse about checking on Foster. That only left Tevin, Cassie, and Maddie. Tevin stayed because Cassie hadn't left, but he didn't know why Maddie stuck around.

"You might not want to believe it, but he's the only one who will have the answer."

"I get why you think that, but you're crazy if you think he'll put his self-interests aside for ours."

"You mean yours. Not ours. The shifters have their own interests, separate from witches." Sybil looked as though she was going to throttle him.

"No, I mean ours, your granddaughter's involved now. So that makes it ours."

"Not yet. She might know why she came here, but she can still walk away."

For the first time since the argument between Sybil and Mac began, Tevin was scared about where it would lead.

He reached for Cassie's hand. Yeah, he knew she could always walk away. It used to keep him awake some nights. He thought about what he might do if she left and both he and his wolf agreed that he'd follow her. He would give up the Broken Peak Pack for her, but he wouldn't give up her for the pack.

She wove her fingers through his and squeezed his hand. Not that he could decipher the meaning behind her hand squeeze, but it eased some of the unease that had reared its ugly head when Sybil gave words to all of Tevin's fears.

Mac looked over at Tevin then back to Sybil. "You really think that's likely?"

For the first time in an hour, Sybil didn't have an answer.

"That's what I thought." Mac stood and circled the table while stretching his arms over his head before sitting back down next to Sybil. "He's obsessed with the balance, Sybil."

"He was the one who told me to send Cassandra here. He also told me that I should plan on coming to War as well."

"Wait, you've been here? Since when?" Cassie's hand squeezed Tevin's hand hard enough for him to wince. But he didn't pull away.

"Since before your incident with the shifter."

Maddie snorted and Tevin agreed with her sentiment. What happened with the hyena shifter didn't qualify as an incident under anyone's definition.

"How come I didn't know? Why didn't you tell me?"

"The Book."

"You know where you can put that book, Memaw?" Cassie stood, but Tevin pulled her back down into his lap.

"I was here, just in case. And it looks like we've reached the just in case portion." Sybil ignored her granddaughter's outburst and looked at Tevin. "Except I can't help with this just in case and no one trusts the one who probably can."

"For what it's worth, he hasn't done anything to make me think we can't trust him." Maddie spoke using her calming doctor's tone. The one that demanded cooler heads prevail. Why she hadn't used it sooner, Tevin didn't know, but planned on finding out. Shortening the argument by even ten minutes would have been better for everyone involved.

Sybil took a deep breath and smiled with a lifetime of wisdom at Maddie. "He killed the Great Shifters. He destroyed every last one of them. And now, a Great Shifter has emerged, after eons of believing them to be extinct? It's hard to trust his motives. For all we know, he might just be waiting for Cassandra to get here and become the final piece, then destroy them all."

"Memaw, you just switched arguments." Cassie sighed and closed her eyes in frustration.

"No, I am explaining why there is distrust." Sybil looked over at Cassie for a moment before turning to Mac. "I don't trust him either, but he's the only one who might have the answer without us spending days if not weeks looking for it. For all we know this might be a new breed of supernaturals."

"You think he'd tell us if it was? He's still denying any involvement with the mindwipers."

"I think that's based on a technicality. He owned up to the sympaths and empaths though."

"What are sympaths and empaths?" Tevin wasn't sure he wanted to know, but he asked anyway.

"They can manipulate and gain energy from emotions. empaths are mostly benign, but sympaths especially feed off of negative emotions." Sybil leveled that wise gaze of hers at him. "But they have to be close to the person, and Mac would have seen him if your visitor was a sympath or empath."

Maddie sighed and pushed away from the table. "We've been through all these books and the reasons why we shouldn't ask Alexander for help. I just don't see how we're going to get the answer of what the man was without Alexander's help."

After Sybil explained the reason for the distrust, he was more concerned about Cassie than he had been right after he learned about the hyena shifter. Plus, it kind of felt like once Alexander showed up, things might get a lot more permanent and things would turn to Cassie not being able to leave. Not that he wanted her to leave, in fact, if he had his way she'd stay around forever. But he wanted her to *want* to stay. Like when she kissed him at the store. Cassie didn't do it because she wanted something from him. She didn't do it to distract him, which he really didn't mind. She hadn't even kissed him because he asked her to. Cassie kissed him because she wanted to.

"Mac, we aren't going to be able to figure this out unless we expand the search, but that means letting outsiders know what's happening. Is that better than asking for Alexander's help?"

"Thirty minutes. If we can't figure it out in thirty minutes, we'll contact him." Mac grabbed one of the books they had already looked through two hours earlier.

"Who's going to tell Vixen?" Sybil asked.

"She'll figure it out soon enough now that you've stopped arguing." Maddie pulled a book closer and flipped through the pages. "Edna really was a kook, Mac."

"Yeah, but that's because she was worried about being caught. So you have to read everything assuming a human has read it already and isn't supposed to understand what she wrote down." Mac sighed and rolled his shoulders.

"Eleanor looked through all of this?" Sybil asked.

"Yep. Except for your book, she's been through everything before." Mac grumbled and flipped the page.

"If she couldn't find it, how are we supposed to?" Cassie slid a journal to Tevin and took one for herself.

"Just keep looking." Thirty seconds later Mac pushed his book away. "Who am I kidding? If Eleanor couldn't find it, the rest of us aren't gonna have a better chance."

Mac didn't even last ten minutes before Maddie was on the phone calling Alexander. He got up to find Vixen and Bray and inform them of his decision.

"He's a stubborn curmudgeon."

"People in glass houses, Memaw." Cassie smiled at her grandma, one of the first Tevin had seen from her since Sybil showed up at their door.

"You're on speaker, Alex."

"Hello, Sybil." A male voice came from the phone Maddie put in the center of the table and a pang of jealousy stabbed through Tevin.

That voice was far too confident for Tevin's liking. It belonged to a male who Tevin wanted to stay as far away from Cassie as possible.

"Hello, Alexander." Okay, so there was no love lost between Alexander and Sybil.

"We have a question we think you might be able to answer." Mac jumped in. "Tell him, Tevin."

And so Tevin retold the story about pouncing on a man who wasn't there. A man only he could see. And a man no one sensed.

Alexander didn't even wait for Tevin to finish. "Wizard."

"What? They're all dead?"

"A few survived, I didn't realize any of them came from a line strong enough to project though. That takes a lot of power."

"You can do it." Sybil's tone held nothing but accusation.

"And where do you think I gained that power? But it's not mine to pass on. I assure you." Based on the tone of his voice, if Alexander had been there, he would have been glaring daggers at Sybil. "But there's a bigger problem than what he is, how did he know Cassandra was there?"

"How did that shifter know about Cassandra?" Tevin asked no one in particular.

"The hyena?" Mac asked.

"The one we took care of came from a pack in the southeast." Maddie supplied.

Mac reached toward the phone, likely intending to cut the line off before they gave what he felt would be too much information to Alexander.

"Two ties to Cassandra then?" It was hard to mistake the concern in Alexander's voice for anything else.

"Three. The shifter we found in War who gave us Cassie's name, the hyena, and the wizard, or whatever he was."

And just like that, Tevin's concern for Cassie quadrupled. There was no way in hell she was stepping foot outside the Lodge. Maybe not even outside the bedroom if he had his way.

"They could all be from the same source though, right?" Maddie asked, bringing reason into the conversation.

"I've never heard of a hyena working for a wolf before. Wolves usually stay with their own kind for jobs like these, but there's a first for everything." Tevin answered, and from the look on Cassie's face she was surprised by his knowledge. "I was on my own and without a pack for a while. You learned these things just because loners usually end up hanging around other loners and they all tell stories."

"We're still back where we started, aren't we?" Mac asked.

"I'll reach out to some contacts and see what they know. If I learn anything, I'll let you know." Alexander ended the call.

They all stared at the phone, digesting what they had learned. And what someone would have to tell Vixen and Bray.

"Well, come on then, Sybil, you can keep me company when I go tell Vixen that she's going to owe Alexander a favor." Mac stood and offered his arm to the older witch.

She took it, and they walked together out of the kitchen with their heads close together, talking about something.

"She's hiding something and I'm going to find out what." Cassie glowered at the empty doorway.

Maddie turned, so she faced Cassie and gave her a wide-eyed stare. "Maybe, you should start with yourself. If you want her to tell you everything, you should share all your secrets."

Cassie shifted slightly in his lap and looked down at her hands.

"I have no idea what's going on here, but as long as you do whatever it is you want to do from the Lodge, Cassie, that's fine. Until we can figure out what's going on, you leaving here isn't up for negotiation."

"What?" She sputtered and jumped from his lap to her feet. "Why am I suddenly in lock down?"

"You sat here during the entire conversation, what part of it didn't you understand? That whoever is attacking us might be coming after you specifically? Or that they might be using you to get to us?" Tevin's fear pushed the anger in his voice, and his wolf's anxiety wasn't helping matters. "So, no, you aren't leaving here. End of discussion."

Cassie planted her hands on her hips, ready to deliver what Tevin was sure to be a scathing retort when Maddie interrupted.

"You also need to consider your health. It's not the best decision for you to be wandering about from a medical perspective."

"Yeah, see, what she said." Tevin stood and circled the table closing the distance between him and Cassie. "I'm just worried about you, Cassie, I want you safe and healthy. Okay?"

Cassie stood there for all of three seconds before shaking her head and storming out the kitchen. Except instead of going to the front room and out the front door in the act of defiance Tevin expected, she turned left and headed to their bedroom.

Their?

Yep. He said it. And he meant it. Their bedroom. It wasn't his anymore, it was his and Cassie's.

"You know, when I said that thing about being honest, I meant everyone. Tell her how you feel, Tev, before you lose your chance." Maddie stood and left the kitchen, leaving Tevin alone.

CHAPTER TWENTY-ONE

IN THE past seventy-two hours, Broken Peak had gone through some major changes.

The first was Eleanor, Danielle, Maggie, and Foster leaving to stay with Memaw in the house she had secured. Suffice it to say, once Cassandra learned her grandma had rented out the mansion and used her magic, she hadn't been pleased. If Cassandra had stayed at the mansion instead, maybe none of the events that led to the near evacuation of the Broken Peak Pack from their home would have happened. The mansion was deemed safe only because as far as they could tell, Sybil Voisin's presence in War was still unknown. Cassandra understood why Vixen and Bray made the decision. She would have probably made the same decision were she in their place. It also didn't hurt that Mac vouched for her grandma, pointing out that if she managed to keep Cassandra alive and well for over twenty years then she was more than capable of keeping the humans and pup safe with the help of a raccoon shifter.

Maggie being a raccoon shifter was news to Cassandra, but it did explain the female's attraction to shiny clothes. Memaw had assured Cassandra that Maggie was more than just a raccoon shifter and pointed to a passage in one of Mac's old journals. Apparently raccoon shifters had a lot more magic in them than anyone, even other shifters, realized.

The second big change was that all the males and Vixen were either out on patrol or in War, hoping to uncover the why behind the latest attacks. That meant Cassandra was stuck inside the lodge. Tevin did his best to keep someone with her, probably to keep her from going crazy and making a run for it. And for the most part, that meant Finley, Maddie, or Tevin got stuck with babysitting duty. But sometimes the baby sitting schedule had holes.

As was the current case.

"Tevin will be here in forty-five minutes, Cassandra." Maddie stared at her from just outside the front door. "You're not going to do anything foolish, right?"

She rolled her eyes and said nothing. After the first night of the new lock down, she came to an unsettling conclusion. If she ran, everyone, including her grandma, would find her and her cage, no matter how gilded, would become much smaller.

Maddie sighed and Cassandra tilted her head to the side, knowing there would be a second chastisement.

There always was.

"Cassandra, you need to tell him. If you trusted him enough to share everything, maybe he wouldn't insist you have someone watching you."

"Sure, I'm supposed to trust him after he grabbed me from my hotel and always has me in his sight. I can't even go to the bathroom without him knowing."

"Are you really that miserable?"

"Maybe it's Stockholm Syndrome."

"Nice try. Your grandma was right, you'd be terrible at poker."

"When did she tell you that?"

"When she gave us a list of your tells to watch out for. Look, I know it sucks, and I know you handled the hyena shifter, but what if that was a fluke? You aren't even sure of how it happened." Maddie grinned. "It's not all that bad, right? You have an espresso maker to take care of your small daily allotment of caffeine, and Danielle said she loaded a bunch of books onto an ereader for you. And you even have a phone you can use, now."

"Yeah, but I can only dial the numbers already in the contact list."

Maddie laughed then tried to hide it with a cough. "Who else would you call?"

"I have friends. Up north."

"And what are you going to say? Hey, guess what? I'm a witch and I slept with a wolf shifter and now I'm pregnant?"

Maddie had a point. Okay, she had several points. But Cassandra wasn't ready to admit her feelings for Tevin to anyone else yet. It was bad enough that she battled with all of it on a daily basis, but what was worse is that she really wasn't bothered by half of what she complained about.

And Tevin definitely didn't bother her. Sure, he annoyed her and could piss her off, but she really didn't want to leave him behind.

So she put up a fight for appearance's sake, and Maddie saw right through it. Cassandra was lucky that Tevin wasn't nearly as observant.

"Fine. I'll behave. I swear." She crossed her fingers over her heart.

"You're going to have to tell him soon, Cassandra. He's going to figure it out. As oblivious as Tevin can be, he'll definitely notice when your body starts to change and your boobs get bigger."

"I'll blame the cronuts." She had to get Maddie to leave, or she'd get caught. She wasn't planning on leaving, or doing anything stupid, but she just needed a break. "I'll tell him. But right now he's being punished for deciding that I need babysitting."

"But weren't you punishing him for taking you from the hotel? Maddie asked.

"Yes. And because Tevin's who he is, I'm sure there will be another reason to punish him."

"You know there are better ways to punish him than not telling him he's going to be a father. I found the silent treatment to be effective and when all else fails, withhold sex."

"I'll behave, I promise. Just go, Maddie." Cassandra added a smile to her words, hoping it would ease some of her friend's concerns.

She stood in the open doorway for a few more seconds. "I wish I could get you to promise to tell him as easily as you promise to not do a runner."

"I said I'd tell him. After his time in the penalty box is over." Cassandra grinned. "Now close the door so you can hear me lock it behind you."

Maddie shook her head and laughed, closing the door so Cassandra could do what she promised and lock the door.

After counting to sixty, twice, Cassandra ran to the bedroom. She'd realized relatively quickly that if Tevin knew just how angry she was about the lock down, he'd never give her any room to breathe.

Besides, she'd already come to terms that she wasn't going to walk away from him. She enjoyed the way his body cocooned around her when she woke up in the mornings, keeping her warm and safe. But even better was when they fell asleep together and his breath danced over her skin, a silent reminder that he'd always be there.

She even enjoyed the angry sex they had after he decided she wasn't going to leave Broken Peak until they solved the current problem. After waking up in an empty bed in the middle of the night, she found him stretched out on the couch in the front room. She brought him back to the bedroom and then because apparently she couldn't control herself or her vagina when it came to Tevin, they fucked. There was no other way to describe it. And yeah, it was angry sex, and not very healthy, she got that, but it was amazing. Tevin might have believed it was more along the lines of make-up sex, and Cassandra let him believe that. Not that she was proud about anything she did that night. But if she wanted to survive the lock down with her sanity intact, she had to convince everyone she was on board. Even if it was reluctantly, so they didn't get too suspicious.

What she didn't enjoy was his over protectiveness. Or when he made decisions on her behalf. Which he didn't do all that much, but the few times he had, it pissed her off. But she also needed alone time. And she needed time with Memaw and maybe some of the other females in the pack, without Tevin hovering a few feet away. But what she needed most was time with the magic that was close to the earth.

Once in the room, she pulled on a pair of low boots that tied and grabbed a sweater. She promised Maddie she'd behave and not do a runner, but she needed to feel the sun on her face and the earth beneath her feet. She wanted to talk with the magic that was waiting just outside the door for her. There was plenty of magic she could tap inside the lodge, but it wasn't anything like the magic swirling around outside.

Okay, so she felt a pinch guilty about her subterfuge. But only a little. So she pushed it aside while doing her best not to tell Maddie an outright lie.

Besides, Cassandra only planned on spending a few minutes outside. And then she would come right back inside and sit on the couch reading something when Tevin walked through the door.

She ran through the lodge to the front room, almost crashing into the door as she slid to a stop, so she could unlock it before stepping outside. With the last lock undone, she threw the door open and stepped outside. She took a deep breath of the fresh air. And then a second and third before jogging down the porch steps to the yard and letting the magic greet her.

Except as soon as she stood on the ground, there was nothing. The magic was there, she could feel it, but she couldn't touch it.

Cassandra tried to call to it, but something was off. Like there was a barrier between her and the magic preventing them from communicating with each other.

"So, the little witch they stashed away came out to play."

Cassandra spun to her right and faced the source of the voice. A man, one she didn't know and didn't recognize, stood a few feet away.

His dark greasy hair fell to his shoulders in clumps and his dark eyes squinted, as though he wasn't used to the sun. And there was something else way off with him. He didn't feel right. Everything about him was off, as though he wasn't in the right skin.

Whoever he was, he didn't belong at Broken Peak.

She turned and ran for the lodge. If she could just get to the door. She didn't even make it three steps before her head jerked back. The man grabbed her hair and wasn't gentle. He yanked her back, upending her balance, and she struggled to not fall over.

"You can't run away, little witch."

She kicked back, but either he was ready for the move or her aim was way off, because her foot only hit empty air.

Cassandra called the magic to her, but it wouldn't listen. Or maybe it didn't even hear her.

She screamed. She opened her mouth and released all the air from her lungs.

Not that anyone was close enough to hear. But maybe, if she was lucky, someone's patrol led them close enough to the lodge.

The man's fist swung into her stomach, hard enough to leave her gasping for breath. Cassandra hit the ground, and she curled forward, wrapping her arms around her stomach.

The fear she had for herself shifted to her baby.

His fist slammed into her temple and her face slammed into the ground. Blood seeped from her nose and stars danced in front of her eyes.

She could continue to fight, but it would just end with her being hurt. Or worse, the baby. And that was if she was lucky. Something inside of her pulled back the instinct to fight. Just do what he said, go along with it and her baby--*their* baby--would be safe.

Tevin would find her.

He'd come and get her.

Tevin would save her.

She snapped her mouth closed and curled into a tight ball, protecting her stomach with her arms.

"You're a fast learner, little witch." He grabbed her arm and dragged her across the yard to the woods.

Once he reached the line marking the yard from the trees, she saw her death flash in front of her. He waved a knife, one with a sharp blade and meant for causing damage to whatever it entered, in front of her face.

"You're gonna be good, or I'm going to cut your tendon. I'll let you bleed out while I take what I want from you and I'll make it painful. Or maybe, I'll let you die slowly from hundreds of cuts and still take what I want.

She must have stared at the knife for too long, because the man kicked her shoulder hard. When Cassandra finally looked at his sneering face, she flinched away. But not fast enough before his palm came down hard on her cheek, sending a new wave of stars to her eyes.

"Stand up."

Taking as much time as she could to get to her feet, she tried to come up with a plan. Anything that would keep her baby safe. And alive.

She looked over her shoulder, back at the yard, wishing Tevin was back earlier than planned. He would have known what to do. Tevin would have been able to save her from the lunatic.

But her wish didn't come true.

The man pushed her and she stumbled forward. Except instead of her foot landing on the ground, it landed on a cement floor.

One second she had been at Broken Peak the next she was in what looked like an old warehouse. The lunatic had magic she'd never seen or even heard about before.

Cassandra spun around, hoping that whatever doorway she had gone through was still there. It was gone. But the man wasn't.

It took everything she had not to cry. She would not let him see the tears. No. She *couldn't* let him.

"You're going to be a good little witch. I'd hate to have to hurt you sooner than planned." A maniacal grin accompanied his words.

He pushed her into a small room without any windows or lights and locked the door.

Cassandra cried. She cried for her baby. She cried for herself. She cried for Tevin. For not knowing he was going to be a father. For not knowing how she felt about him. She cried because she never told Tevin she loved him.

She cried until there were no more tears left and she couldn't cry anymore.

CHAPTER TWENTY-TWO

AS TEVIN approached the yard in front of the Lodge, he recognized the woman racing from the side of the yard to the front door.

Sybil. Cassie's grandma.

He hurried across the yard at a flat run. "Sybil? What the fuck are you doing here and not back at the place you're staying?"

"She's not here!" The older woman stopped at the steps and spun to face Tevin. "She's gone, Tevin. She's not here. What happened? What did you say to her?"

What did Sybil mean about Cassie not being there? Had she gone for a walk as soon as Maddie left? He loved her independent streak, but her disobedience annoyed the fuck out of him. Maybe it was time to threaten her with another spanking.

He took a deep breath, taking a few seconds to calm down before gently pushing Sybil aside and walking to the door. "She should be inside."

The door wasn't locked.

The only reason for the door being unlocked was because Cassie wasn't inside.

But she wouldn't have run. She didn't have anywhere to go.

Tevin pushed the door open and stepped inside. "Cassie!"

He expected her to yell back at him, letting him know where she was, but all he got was silence. He took another step inside, not knowing what he would find.

He called her name again, even though he knew she wasn't inside. He stomped across the room to the hallway with Sybil right behind his every fucking step. She was like a fucking shadow.

"Cassie!"

"Cassandra, sweetheart?"

More silence.

Tevin spun around in the hallway and headed back outside, pulling out his gun. Something had to have happened to Cassie. With his free hand, he took out his phone. "Maddie, she's fucking gone."

He ended the call before Maddie could ask any questions. Tevin prowled in front of the porch looking for any signs. It was only when he made a second pass in front of the porch when he realized his shadow was missing.

Shit. He didn't have time to worry about Sybil. He spun around scanning the yard for her, expecting her to be halfway to the woods, but she stood, frozen in place, just in front of the steps. She was staring at the ground.

Tevin hurried over to her and followed her gaze with his. A few inches in front of her feet he discovered what stopped her in her tracks.

Blood.

Not much, but enough.

Sybil lifted her head and stared at him. He knew her thoughts even before she gave them voice. It was Tevin's job to keep her safe and he failed. He held up his hand, stopping the accusations before they started, belatedly realizing the gun was still in his hand.

She flinched away from the weapon, but her eyes held a hardness and anger he'd never seen before on any woman.

"Sybil..."

"What happened, Tevin? Did you decide you didn't want a baby chaining you to her and figured you could get rid of her then blame it on someone else?"

Baby?

What. The. Fuck?

Tevin stepped back, away from Sybil. Then another step back. Maybe he hoped a wall or chair would miraculously appear behind him, something to keep him from falling over. He fell to his knees.

Baby?

Cassie was *pregnant*?

With *his* baby?

Everything became clear as the pieces fell into place. Maddie's visits. The stomach bug that wasn't ever an issue. Not drinking alcohol. The way Maddie evaded questions, but hinted that something was going on.

He pressed his hands against his face and shook his head. "Pregnant?"

"Shit." The curse word coming from Sybil seemed out of place, but Tevin's mind was too far gone to realize it. "She hasn't told you yet."

Tevin looked up at her. Sybil looked like she was torn between yelling at him for letting Cassie get hurt and comforting him. Neither side won. Instead, she loomed over him staring down into his eyes.

He wasn't sure how long they stayed that way, with Tevin rocking side to side and holding his head and Sybil glaring at him with a combination of anger and sympathy in her eyes.

It was longer than they have though, because when Maddie charged into the yard, neither of them had moved.

"How long?" Maddie asked.

Her words didn't make any sense. Tevin's brain wasn't capable of processing them when it was busy dealing with the newfound knowledge that Cassie was pregnant.

She turned to Sybil and focused on her. Tevin could hear the words, but none of them made any sense. Sybil and Maddie might as well have been speaking a foreign language.

Cassie having a baby was the only thought in his mind. He couldn't think about where she was or who had her. If he had, he would have lost it more than he already had.

Sybil and Maddie must have come to an agreement because Maddie knelt in front of him, holding out a flask.

"Drink."

"She's going to have a baby."

"I know." She shoved the flask to his lips. "Drink. Doctor's orders."

Tevin shoved the flask away and its contents spilled, seeping into the ground the same way the earth absorbed Cassie's blood.

A shudder ran through him at the thought of her blood, and he grabbed his head again. He needed to go back and do everything differently. To never have seen Cassie at the Dirty Whistle. Because if he hadn't seen her, he would have only had to deal with losing a woman he never got the chance to know instead of losing the woman he loved and their baby.

Their baby.

"Fuck it, Tevin. You aren't any help to her in your current state, so drink, grow a pair of balls, and we'll find a way to get her back."

The flask returned to his mouth and this time Tevin drank. He finished the contents in a few swallows. Mac's moonshine burned his throat and stomach on the way down, but it also brought him back to the present.

Maddie was right. It was time to man up.

He looked up at the two of them.

"Slapping him would have been better." Sybil glared at him.

He wanted to slap her right back. But she was Cassie's grandma and it wouldn't have ended well. Instead, he narrowed his eyes and stared at his friend.

"When did you know, Maddie?"

"At the hotel. I found some tests in the garbage in the bathroom. She begged me not to tell you. And between the doctor's oath of confidentiality and it being her place to tell you and not mine, I kept silent." She didn't add that Tevin had been the one to tell her that she didn't know him. She offered him her hand. "You can be pissed with me when we get her back. Vixen and Leighton are on their way."

Tevin wrapped his hand around her wrist and used her for leverage to get back to his feet. "The wizard?"

"Only one who'd be able to get through the alarm system Danielle set up."

"How could your pack let this happen? How could you let anything happen to a pregnant woman? I trusted you because shifters have a reputation for their protectiveness."

Maddie snapped, losing her patience with Sybil. But unlike Tevin, who was close to losing it on the old woman, Maddie held her anger back.

"No one knew she was pregnant except for Cassandra, me, you, and one other. And I'm not sure it would make a difference if Tevin knew or not, but you have to stop throwing it around, because until you blurted it out, it didn't matter. And if none of us could sense she was pregnant, then we have to assume the wizard doesn't know either."

"We can't just pretend Cassandra isn't pregnant, like it didn't happen and there's no baby."

"I know that, Sybil, but for fuck's sake, you're making things worse. So either sit down and shut up or help us and keep your opinion to yourself."

Maddie never lost her patience. And she never lost it with someone who was older. Sybil must have really pissed her off, or Tevin was seeing things and still stuck in the world of the fairies.

She turned her attention back to Tevin. "Let's start with where we know he isn't. Assuming he's in War, he won't be in any of the redone buildings. They're all owned by Alexander. He'd know."

"Call him." Sybil demanded.

Tevin was about to tell her to keep quiet, but Maddie already had her phone out and was dialing. She must have turned on the speaker phone because they all heard it ringing.

"Yes?"

"We think the wizard has Cassie." Tevin blurted out. "Can you think of where he might have taken her?"

Silence.

No one spoke or even so much as breathed, waiting for Alexander's answer.

When it still hadn't come nearly a minute later, Sybil grabbed the phone from Maddie's hand.

"Look, you interfering asshole, this is not a matter of maintaining the balance or whatever you want to call it. This is my granddaughter. My granddaughter who's pregnant. So if you know anything at all, you better say something or I swear, I will hunt you down and find a way to destroy you."

"I can't be of any help right now."

"What do you mean you can't help right now?" Maddie stared at the phone in Sybil's hand. "Why not now?"

"I want Cassandra back at Broken Peak and part of the pack as much as the rest of you. But it's impossible for me to help you right now." Alexander paused for a moment, as though he was considering something, before continuing. "Sybil?"

"Yes?"

"I'm going to bring you all to me, but I need you to bind everyone together. Can you do that?"

Sybil rolled her eyes at Alexander's question. "Of course."

Before Tevin could ask what binding entailed, a surge of magic, like the magic he felt the day he learned Cassie was a witch, surged through him.

And then he was no longer standing in the yard in front of the Lodge. Instead, he stood in the center of a dark room and his stomach was somewhere near his feet.

"Well that was..."

Unpleasant, uncomfortable, never happening again. Tevin finished Maddie's sentence in his mind.

Someone turned on a lamp and in the dim light Tevin realized the room didn't have any windows. The furniture was nice and probably expensive, but none of that mattered.

The man sitting in a high-backed armchair with glowing red eyes and fucking fangs took precedence. Alexander was a fucking vampire. An honest hand-to-God vampire.

"We'll have time for questions and answers later." Alexander cut through their surprise. "Now, someone call Vixen before she accuses me of kidnapping you and I have to deal with her griffin."

Tevin fell back in the chair behind him. He couldn't stop staring at Alexander's elongated canines. Sybil was staring too, just as surprised by the revelation. Maddie was the only one who didn't seem surprised. And she was also the one who called Vixen. Or at least Tevin assumed it was Vixen since she spoke quietly with whoever answered and never put the phone on speaker.

"Sit down already Sybil. Frankly, I'm disappointed in your shock, I thought you had figured it out."

"The Voisins weren't at the Concord."

"Yes, yes. I know. I was there. Remember."

Tevin closed his eyes and took a deep breath while his stomach climbed its way back up his body from his feet. "Cassie. How do we find Cassie?"

Alexander leaned back in his chair and crossed one leg over the other. "He's not staying at The Old Jail. And I doubt he's at any of the motels. He'd know that would be the first place you'd look."

"Danielle? I'm putting you on speaker phone. Sybil, Tevin, and Alexander are here." Maddie placed the phone on the table in front of Alexander and gave Tevin a shrug. "Vixen recommended we use Danielle's computer skills to help narrow down the locations."

He wasn't about to turn away any help, especially the kind of help Danielle could give. "We don't think he's staying at any of the motels in town."

"I'm also eliminating any of the buildings sold in the past eleven weeks." Danielle added. "Do I need to extend that time frame?"

"Twelve weeks. I bought this house three months ago."

Alexander answered before Tevin could ask why she even wanted to know.

"Okay, that leaves... forty-five commercial buildings and a hundred and eighty-one residences."

"Remove any building that had taxes paid prior to December. I've already investigated them."

"Twenty houses and fifteen commercial buildings."

"Remove all residences. He'd want something without neighbors." Maddie added.

Tevin's mind immediately jumped to exactly why he wouldn't want neighbors. His wolf growled and raised his hackles.

"I swear, if he's fucking hurt her, Maddie."

"I know. But let's figure out where he'd go first." Maddie glared at Sybil, stopping her from adding anything.

Tevin didn't need her telling him what he already knew. If the wizard had Cassie, the blood already confirmed he hurt her. He was going to fucking kill the wizard. And he was going to enjoy every minute of it. He'd enjoy the feel of his wolf's teeth ripping out the wizard's throat and watching as he bled out and took his final breath. And most of all, he'd enjoy watching the wizard's life come to an end.

Maddie looked over at Sybil. "Could you do whatever it's called, the scrying thing, to find him? Cassandra mentioned she used it before."

"Scrying for Cassandra would work, yes, but don't you think we would have done that already?" Alexander leveled his red-eyed gaze on Maddie and Tevin flinched, even though the stare wasn't meant for him. "First, he's probably put up wards and for him to do what he's done, he's powerful enough to feel any kind of magic pushing against those wards. Even if he doesn't have wards up, he'd know the minute Sybil so much as breathed Cassandra's name into the spell. And second, if he knows we're close to him, he'll get rid of her and run. If he hasn't already."

"Cassie is not dead." Tevin growled out through clenched teeth. He refused to consider Cassie not being alive, and he wasn't going to let anyone else think those thoughts. "Don't put shit like that out there."

Sybil bent forward and took a deep breath. Apparently it was her turn to fall apart. Maddie moved to join Sybil on the couch and rubbed her back. When she regained her composure, she sat up and looked across the room at Tevin.

"I'm fine now."

"Go splash some cold water on your face." Maddie patted her back.

"Out the door, to the left, third door down." Alexander dismissed Sybil with a wave of his hand.

Tevin expected an argument, but none came. Sybil did as suggested without a protest.

He waited for the sound of a door closing before speaking. "She can't come with us."

"I know." Maddie rolled her eyes at him.

"Alexander, are you coming with us?" Tevin looked over at the vampire.

"Of course."

"So what do we do with Sybil?"

"Danielle, call Vixen. Let her know we're going to need someone to babysit." Tevin pinched the bridge of his nose between his thumb and forefinger.

Maddie's words from before, when Sybil was yelling at him in front of the Lodge, came into his mind with a rush. Maddie said one other person. Someone else knew Cassie was pregnant and Tevin would bet his life that it was Vixen. No wonder she'd been so understanding about him bringing Cassie to the Lodge.

He'd deal with Maddie sharing the news with Vixen before she shared it with him later. After they got Cassie back.

"Danielle, look at warehouses and start with the ones currently for sale." Tevin looked over at Alexander. "How long until sunset?"

"Thirty minutes. That should give Vixen enough time to find a babysitter and get them here. If they're fast."

"You can't pull them here, like you did with us?"

"Shifters have different magic than the others. It's why I had Sybil bind you together." Alexander patiently explained.

"I found three. Tevin, I'm sending you the addresses. Pick which one you want to take then Vixen and the others will hit the other two. Oh, and Mac's on his way. He should be there shortly."

"I fear my secret lair is no longer quite so secret." Alexander mused.

"Hasn't been for a month."

CHAPTER TWENTY-THREE

WITHOUT any light, Cassandra wasn't sure where she was. There wasn't any furniture, so she huddled in the corner with her back pressed against the wall. At least her nose stopped bleeding, but her cheek throbbed and her right eye was swollen shut.

She pulled up her knees, using her legs as a shield for her stomach, and stared at the door while waiting for the maniac to come back.

Cassandra told herself over and over that Tevin would find her. They'd realize she hadn't run and would be looking for her. Why hadn't she left a clue or something? In all the movies, the woman always left behind some item only the hero would recognize. Then he'd figure it out in record time, barge through the door, and save the day. Usually right at the last minute. But he always saved the day.

Crap.

Cassandra didn't want a last minute rescue. She wanted a right now rescue. No. Scratch that. She wanted a five minutes ago rescue.

The tears threatened to escape again, but she held them back. Crying wouldn't help her find a way out, and it might actually make the lunatic happy. There wasn't really a reason for her to believe crying would please him, except the grin on his face when he looked at her.

To him, she wasn't a person. She was a little witch. A toy he would eventually break then throw away.

She dropped her head to her knees and closed her eyes. Things could only get worse, and she needed to keep their baby safe.

Her magic wasn't working. She had tried to call for it as soon as he closed the door, but got nothing. She couldn't even sense it. Words probably would help either. She hadn't recognized anything close to logic and reason during the short time he'd spoken with her. Strength was out too. He might be thin and wiry, but he hit her with more force than she expected.

Intelligence was her best option and that meant escape. Except she wasn't in a computer game where she could collect a pile of unconnected items and figure out how to get out of a locked room.

On the plus side she was still breathing. And breathing was better than not breathing.

She hugged her legs closer to her chest and wished Tevin was with her. But no matter how hard she wished, she didn't imagine him breaking through the door and saving her. She hoped it would happen. Even prayed for it. But whenever she closed her eyes, it wasn't Tevin she saw barging into the room. It was the wizard.

Cassandra pressed closer to the wall and savored the surrounding silence. As long as it was quiet, she was alone and the crazy ass wizard wasn't tormenting her. He might have been planning on what he'd do to her. But as long as she was alone, Cassandra was safe. Their baby was safe.

Crap. She needed to get out of here.

She looked around the small room for the hundredth time. Even though it was dark and her eyes had somewhat adjusted to light. Enough for her to see that the room was bare. She stared at the door, willing herself not to think about what might happen, and focus on what she could do instead.

Not much.

But Cassandra wasn't surrendering without at least trying.

Wait. The hinges. They were on the inside. The door opened *into* the room.

If she could get the pins out, she could make a run for it. But she needed to make sure he wasn't around or at least far enough away, so he couldn't catch her. If he caught her, he'd kill her right away. Of that, she was certain.

No longer sitting in the corner of the room waiting for something to happen, she felt slightly better. Not much, but at least now she was waiting to *do* something.

"No words, little witch? You must not want to be saved." The wizard's voice taunted her from outside the door, but at least the lunatic hadn't come into the room.

Except she wasn't sure if that was good or bad. She couldn't antagonize him. That much she knew. If Cassandra antagonized him, he'd have his reason to do whatever he planned for her.

The voice that told her not to fight, to keep their baby safe was the same voice telling her not to say anything or encourage him. So that's what she did. She bit her tongue and said nothing.

As long as she didn't engage with him, he'd grow bored toying with her and go back to whatever he was doing before. Or at least that's what she hoped would happen.

He cackled through the door. "Don't fret little witch. You'll find your words soon enough."

The sound of his voice combined with his words sent a wave of dread through her. But still, Cassandra said nothing. Not because she didn't want to antagonize him, but because she knew if she opened her mouth again, the tears would start. And then he'd know that his words were working.

She wanted Tevin to save her, but what if he wasn't looking for her?

Cassandra gave her mind a kick.

She needed to save herself. She had to gather her wits and get the hell out of there. If not for her then for the baby.

Her gaze settled on the hinges as she tuned out the noises coming from the other side of the door.

The hinges were the key to her freedom.

CHAPTER TWENTY-FOUR

SYBIL glared at Tevin from her perch on the chair across the room. Mac was standing just behind her, ready to pounce if she so much as shifted her weight. "Are you going to get our girl?"

What did she think? That Tevin was an idiot? Yeah, he lost his shit, but that was because he had just learned Cassie was pregnant. All things considered, he probably would have lost his shit no matter what else was going on when he learned Cassie was pregnant. With *his* baby.

Sybil didn't budge. She hadn't moved since Mac arrived and pushed her into her chair. They hadn't resorted to physically restraining her, but they hadn't removed it from their options.

"Well are you?"

Tevin left the room and ignored her question. Maddie and Alex followed, but Mac stayed with Sybil.

They waited until they left the room before stopping by Alexander's personal arsenal, which gave the room at Broken Peak a run for its money. While they grabbed enough weapons to take out an army of wizards, Tevin looked over at the vampire.

"You figure out which warehouse?"

"Fairly sure."

"Fairly?" Tevin didn't want to hear the word fairly. He preferred absolutes. If they went to the wrong warehouse, it would be time wasted and Tevin wasn't willing to waste even a second finding Cassie. That meant going in when they were certain.

"One of my contacts says it doesn't have any earth magic. But earth magic doesn't behave that way."

Tevin blinked slowly at Alexander. Until a few weeks ago, Tevin didn't believe magic, outside of the magic that lived within shifters, existed.

Alexander sighed. "Earth magic exists everywhere. There are some places with more magic than others, but it's impossible for magic to completely avoid a place. Unless someone was blocking the magic."

"And your friend thinks someone is blocking the magic?"

"Contact. He doesn't think, he knows. But we don't know who is blocking the magic. It might be the wizard we're after, or it may be another wizard. He didn't want to investigate in case the wizard got spooked."

Alexander's words made sense. Not that Tevin enjoyed hearing them, but they made sense. "How can we be sure?"

"We can't."

Tevin glared at Maddie. That wasn't the answer he wanted to hear.

"It's improbable there's a second wizard in War who is strong enough to shield magic. Not impossible, but improbable. So, no, we can't be certain, Tevin. But he was arrogant enough to show up in a pack's territory and wasn't worried about getting caught. I'm not sure he's worried he'll be caught now. And that's to our advantage." Alexander intervened with logic and reason before Tevin lost it on Maddie.

"And Cassandra's smart. That's good for us too." Maddie added.

Maddie and Alexander looked at Tevin, waiting for him to respond. Except Tevin couldn't find any words. Sure, he had a lot he wanted to say, but nothing that would actually help. And it wouldn't make him feel better either.

"I'm not sure how long Mac can keep Sybil distracted." Alexander packed more guns and ammo into a pack than they'd probably need, but Tevin wasn't complaining. "Once we get outside, you two can shift and I'll take your clothes. Then I'll blink in short hops and you can follow me. It will be the fastest way to get there."

Tevin nodded in agreement. Plus, his wolf had been pushing at him. The run to the warehouse would be good for the beast.

They were going to get Cassie. And if even one hair was out of place, his wolf was going to rip out the wizard's throat. His wolf was going to rip out the wizard's throat anyway.

"I texted Vixen our target. She'll take care of the other two locations." Maddie tossed Alexander her phone.

Tevin was tired of waiting around. He wanted to get his girl. "Let's go."

Alexander nodded and slung the full pack over his shoulders.

They'd have to go in with everything available. No way would that wizard get away from them. And if Tevin's wolf had his way, it would be nice and messy.

They needed to deliver a message and it had to be loud enough for every supernatural to hear it. Cassie was Tevin's and anyone who so much as looked at her the wrong way would not be long for the world.

The mates of the Broken Peak Pack were protected.

Mate?

Mate.

His wolf confirmed what had been lingering in the back of Tevin's mind since that first night at the Dirty Whistle. Cassie was his mate. She was the mother of his child. And he'd spend the rest of his life arguing with her about it if he had to.

They moved as a group to the front door. At the last second, just before stepping outside, Tevin glanced over his shoulder.

Sybil stood in the doorway of the room they'd left her in with Mac hovering just behind her.

"Tevin. Once you find her, kill him. Because if you fail, I won't. And I will make it a hundred times worse for the bastard." The words coming from the older woman surprised him. "No one hurts my girl and lives."

From behind Sybil, Mac rolled his eyes and shook his head, but kept quiet. So did Tevin.

He just nodded then turned and stepped through the front door. The others waited for him just a few feet away.

"I've spent a lot of years dealing with Sybil. She's a force of her own making. You sure Cassandra's worth that?" Alexander asked with a raised eyebrow and the hint of a smirk.

Tevin ignored the question and stripped off his clothes then handed them to the vampire. With as much tension and anxiety coursing through him, Tevin had been concerned it would take a moment before he could shift. He didn't need to be. His wolf pushed Tevin aside and took over.

No lights flashed and nothing sparkled. One second Tevin was there and the next his wolf stood on the ground, legs splayed for balance while he shook out his body.

Normally when Tevin shifted, he surrendered everything to the wolf. Not this time. He slid into the wolf's mind, and the beast allowed it. As though he not only expected it, but wanted it.

The wolf howled at the moon and Maddie's mountain lion echoed it with a scream. The vampire chuckled.

"Let's go." The vampire winked at the animals. Then with a small flash of light that might have had a glimpse of sparkles to it, Alexander disappeared.

It took all of thirty seconds before the wolf caught the scent of the vampire and took off. Swallowing the ground beneath his feet as he ran across the land to his target. At the rate they were moving, it would be at least thirty minutes before they made it to the warehouse. And if they were wrong and Cassie wasn't there, Tevin wasn't sure what they would do.

His wolf was sure though. They'd keep on looking. And when they found her, because nothing else was an option, they'd bring her back to the Lodge and the pack where they'd keep her safe. For the rest of their lives.

As soon as they found the vampire, he blinked away, and they followed after him. While his wolf ran, Tevin had time to think. Which wasn't good, especially when his wolf's mind was focused on finding Cassie. Vixen's words from the conversation that started everything came back to him. *If something happens to me or Bray, you're the one most capable of making the decisions that will need to be made.*

He thought he understood what she meant at the time, but it wasn't until then, with Cassie's life on the line and the danger coming from a wizard with unknown powers, that he fully comprehended Vixen's meaning.

If Maddie or Alexander died while saving Cassie, Tevin would mourn their death, but he wouldn't change things. Same went for the others. If they died while attempting a rescue, Tevin would be sad, but he wouldn't regret it.

The decisions that needed to be made in the future, assuming the wizard was a hint of what was to come, might mean friends died.

Thankfully, Vixen and Bray would be making most of those decisions, but there might come a time when Tevin had to. And he'd do it. He'd make those difficult decisions because they would be what was best for the pack.

His wolf silently agreed with Tevin's thoughts.

After the fourth disappearing and chasing leg of the trip, they found Alexander in an alley between two rundown brick buildings that might have been filled with night-shift workers in another time. Before War lost its factories to cheaper labor.

The vampire looked over at the wolf. "I assume you'll want to stay as you are?"

The wolf's tail wagged in agreement.

Maddie had already shifted back and was pulling on her clothes. Alexander handed her the pack once she was dressed and checked his own weapons.

The wolf circled around them, wanting to move. Staying still meant they were losing valuable seconds.

"Let me go in first." Alexander didn't ask, he commanded.

Tevin understood it, even if his wolf didn't. The vampire didn't intend to take Tevin's kill. Alexander was protecting Tevin from what they might find once inside the warehouse.

His wolf growled.

Yeah, he couldn't think like that. They would find Cassie and she'd be fine. Everything would be fine. Because if they didn't, he wasn't sure what his wolf would do. Fuck. Tevin wouldn't know what *he* would do.

The wizard would die though.

No matter what.

It was time to make an announcement to all supernaturals. Those they knew about and those they didn't. The world of the supernaturals was changing. Either stand with the females of the Broken Peak Pack or stand against them and be destroyed.

"Let's go." Alexander led with the wolf and Maddie right behind him in a wedge formation.

The vampire paused at the back of the building, but the wolf pushed past him. They weren't slinking in through the back door. The warehouse had to have a front door, and they were going to blast their way in.

Alexander appeared directly in front of the wolf, but didn't stop. He must have done that blinking thing. Good. At least he hadn't tried to stop the wolf. The sound of Maddie's racing steps came from behind, but he didn't look back.

They were too close now to slow down.

The front of the building held a massive steel door, probably used for loading trucks, and two smaller doors on either side.

Alexander ignored the smaller doors. He pressed his palms against the steel and closed his eyes. After a few seconds, he stepped back and stared at the door. Tevin hadn't a clue what was happening, and his wolf didn't either. But his wolf trusted the vampire.

The door screamed, as though it was bending in on itself, then tore free from its hinges and flew into the warehouse. Like someone had thrown it.

Well fuck.

So much for the element of surprise.

As the door crashed down on the cement floor a scream tore through the warehouse.

Cassie.

The beast charged into the building, following the noise. And Maddie and Alexander followed the wolf. They wouldn't have been able to stop the wolf if they tried. The man causing that scream needed to die and the wolf was going to make sure of it.

CHAPTER TWENTY-FIVE

THE DOOR to the room crashed open and Cassandra barely moved out of the way before it slammed into her. She pressed her body against the wall and blinked at the silhouette of the man standing in the doorway.

One of the pins was loose enough to slip free, and she'd been working on the second. She had planned on waiting until the last second and had a better chance of escaping before pulling them free. But it looked as though she ran out of time.

There was a chance she'd live through whatever the lunatic had planned, and she held onto it with all she had. She was going to live and so was her baby. No matter what. And she'd see Tevin again, but she couldn't think about that. Thoughts of Tevin were a distraction she didn't need at the moment.

"Who are you?" Cassandra stalled for time.

As long as the wizard was talking then he wasn't doing anything else. She figured out he had a one track mind and when things didn't go according to his plan he turned to violence. The violence combined with his irrationality made for a dangerous recipe and one that didn't bode well for her physical well-being.

"I'm disappointed you don't know who I am." His thin lips cracked into a wide grin revealing crooked yellowed teeth that matched the jaundiced tone of his skin. "But all that will change, little witch. Don't worry, after tonight everyone will know who I am."

Cassandra wasn't thinking about the words coming from her mouth, only that she needed to buy time. "I can help with that. I know people who can help with that. We can make sure everyone knows you."

He wasn't expecting her words, or maybe he didn't hear them. For everything the wizard might have been, sane wasn't anywhere on the list. At least he hadn't hurt her again after locking her in the room.

Yet.

His tongue ran over his lips and Cassandra shivered. He looked like a snake, ready to strike its meal and swallow it whole.

Nothing about the wizard was right. His eyes never focused on one thing and his hands jerked, as if under the control of a puppeteer yanking on strings. He looked sick and his mind didn't appear healthy either.

He was broken.

Not that she hadn't realized how insane he was when he showed up inside the pack's territory and stole her away, but there was a disconnection between his reality and everyone else's reality.

She studied him and the discipline of observation she gained from years of studying spells and magic came back with a rush.

Cassandra couldn't be certain, but she thought his eyes were dilated. She pushed at her memory, trying to bring forward the image of him when he stood in front of her in the yard. Had his pupils taken over most of his irises then too?

Then there was the jaundiced skin and the muscles jerks.

He was either on drugs or something was poisoning him. And both could have been the cause for his madness.

She went back to her latest impression of him. That nothing seemed right.

He licked at the corner of his lips, and she noticed the dry spittle. How had she not seen the crusty flecks before?

A rabid animal. That's what he reminded her of.

As he stepped into the room, he kept his body between her and the door. Cassandra edged closer to the corner. She didn't know how much time had passed since she'd been locked away, but the light coming from the warehouse wasn't natural. It must be nighttime. So either a few hours had passed or an entire day. She hadn't fallen asleep, so she went with hours.

Was that enough time for Tevin to figure out where she was and find her?

He took a step towards her, and she pressed back against the wall, but it didn't give.

His right arm jerked away from his body, and he reached around his chest to pull his arm back in place. Cassandra didn't want to look at his hands, but she couldn't help herself. The same hands that might have given her a concussion. The ones that had punched her stomach. The hands that were going to deliver more pain if she couldn't find a way to stop him.

"You know I'm a witch, but what are you?"

The wizard stopped walking, like he couldn't walk and think at the same time. Or maybe he was surprised she wanted to know.

His left hand twitched, and he blinked rapidly, like he was thinking about the answer. He took another step towards her. "Don't play dumb, little witch."

She pressed against the wall, wishing she could find even a speck of magic to touch, but nothing was there. Just like every other attempt she'd made since he brought her to her prison.

"You have magic, but none I've ever seen before." She tried to stall him again.

"Little witch, it's time you learn you aren't the only magic in this world."

"Then tell me about it."

"The vampire knows about me. You should have listened to him." The word vampire was filled with hate.

Vampire? There were vampires? What was next? Fairies and elves?

But who was the vampire? Alexander? It made sense. So then, maybe the wizard taking Cassandra didn't have anything to do with her or the Broken Peak Pack and those stupid prophecies.

"Alexander? It's not like he represents all the supernaturals. He's just one magical creature in a world filled with them."

As soon as she spoke, she wished she could put the words back into her mouth. She had inadvertently reminded the wizard that he wasn't anyone special either.

He launched for her and grabbed her arms. His grip was stronger than she remembered, and she struggled against him as he dragged her from the small room into the main part of the building. As soon as she saw what he had been working on during her seclusion, she redoubled her efforts to pull away.

A large wooden table, big enough to hold a body, sat in the middle of the space. Dark runes had been etched around the perimeter of the table and thick leather bands had been nailed into its surface. It looked like an ancient device used in torture to hold the victim in place. A small table, just next to the large one, displayed a collection of knives and blades.

She had to get the hell out of there.

The wizard was too strong for her. His magic must have been helping him because it was like he had the strength of a man three times his size as he dragged her across the floor, closer to the tables. When they neared the table, he pulled her in front of him, so she faced him.

She couldn't let him bind her to the table.

Her knee came up hard, and she nailed him in the balls. His hands loosened, not much, but enough. Cassandra twisted away and scrambled in the opposite direction of the table. She didn't know if she was running straight into a dead end. But wherever she was headed, it had to be better than the table.

His hand caught her ankle and she fell forward. She reached out with her hands, stopping her body from crashing down on the hard floor and the cement burned her hands.

Giving up wasn't an option.

Cassandra kicked back and crawled forward, looking for a door or window. Anything she might be able to escape through.

She repeated the words over and over. A mantra of sorts. She couldn't feel any magic, but maybe a tiny bit lingered. And maybe it would listen to her.

Find an exit.

Find an exit.

Find an exit.

And then she saw it. Two doors on either side of a mammoth door large enough for trucks to back up to. They were still so far away, but at least she found the exit. She continued to crawl, pulling against the hand wrapped around her ankle and kicking with her free leg. She stretched, willing her body closer to the doors, but the wizard was too strong.

He dragged her back towards the table. For every foot she gained, she lost two. But still, she refused to give up.

Wood and metal crashed to the floor and the wizard cursed.

The hand on her ankle loosened, and she crawled forward only for the grip to tighten as the wizard pulled her away from the doors and slithered up her back. His weight pushed down on her, pressing her body against the floor, and she struggled to fill her lungs with the necessary oxygen.

If she could just move one foot closer.

"Fucking witch." The wizard's hand came down on her temple again, only this time something else was in his hand. Something heavy.

Lights flashed in her eyes and combined with her lack of oxygen, she worried she'd black out.

But the need to survive refused to surrender.

Just as Cassandra made it forward a half a foot, the wizard lifted off her body and flipped her over to her back.

He straddled her hips and sat up with his arms raised over his head. He was holding something in his hands.

A knife. With its blade pointed down at her body.

She reached up and dug her nails into the flesh of his cheeks then dragged her hands down.

Blood seeped from the streaks her nails had gouged in his skin.

His hand came down against her cheek and nose. Blood spurted from her, and she was sure he'd broken her nose. The pain didn't help her, but the blood didn't help the wizard. He grabbed her wrist, but couldn't get a tight enough grip and she slipped free.

She screamed.

No one might be able to hear her, but she wasn't screaming for help. Her scream was one of rage and anger.

Between the pain and the adrenaline pounding through her body, she pulled her legs up just as he was sitting back up with the knife raised over his head again.

People talk about how time slows. Like during a car accident and knowing it will happen but not being able to stop it. And that's what happened to Cassandra. Time came to a standstill.

Her mind understood what was about to happen and shut everything down.

For whatever reason, her mind played the song that had been on the radio in the bar. She heard the Brothers Osborne singing about a *Dead Man's Curve* through the pounding of her blood in her brain.

Instead of smelling the rancid breath from the wizard, the scent of fresh cronuts teased her.

If she couldn't stop what the wizard was going to do, her brain was going to take her away, to a place far away filled with the best moments of her life.

Like waking up in Tevin's arms and falling asleep with his breath on her skin.

She couldn't save herself, but her mind would do what it could.

Cassandra gave up and went limp.

She didn't register the sound of steel crashing or the loud growl or the weight of the wizard falling away from her.

"Cassie, baby?" Tevin's voice pushed through the rough voice telling her to keep the wolves from the door.

Her mind must have reached deep inside of her to help with her mental escape from her impending death.

"Cassie?"

A wet warmth covered her, despite no longer feeling the weight on top of her. She didn't want to think what the wizard was doing to her and closed her eyes tight.

Strong arms wrapped around her, but instead of the harsh grip of the wizard like she had expected, the arms cradled her and rocked her gently from side to side.

"Cassie, baby, say something."

It was Tevin's voice again.

"Fuck, Alexander, get a rag or towel." Thick fingers stroked her hair. "Come on, Cassie, tell me you're okay. Yell at me for telling you to say something. Tell me I wasn't too late."

There was no way her mind was that good. Either she died or Tevin was really there. He *did* save her. She opened her eyes, but thumbs or fingers pressed down gently.

"Keep them closed, Cassie. Please?"

She tried to push his hands away, but they didn't move.

"There ya go. Always fighting me." Tevin's soft laughter embraced her tighter than his arms. "Cassie, say something. Say anything."

"I don't have a boyfriend." She wasn't sure where the words came from. What she really wanted to say was that she was pregnant. That he was the father. And she loved him. When she opened her mouth, she planned to say just that. Instead, she confessed something that he probably had already assumed during the weeks she spent with him.

"Yes you do." Tevin laughed, the sound vibrating through his body and rumbling against her.

She loved the way it sounded to her ears and pressed closer to him.

A damp cloth brushed over her face and wiped her eyes.

"We should get her out of here, Tev." Maddie's voice came from the side.

Cassandra turned to the sound. Tevin stopped her and turned her face back to him as he washed her face with the towel. "Almost done, Cassie. Then you can open your eyes."

She wanted them to keep talking. Maybe, if they talked about nothing, her mind wouldn't wander.

The crashing of the door.

The growl.

The weight fell away from her, but not before something warm and sticky covered her.

She opened her eyes and the wizard's limp body laid on the ground in a pool of blood. That warm liquid on her was blood. And not her blood. She looked back at the body. His throat was torn out, the flesh ragged where something had chewed through his neck.

The instinct to fight or flee rushed back and she needed to get away. She wanted to run away from all of it.

Tevin's arms tightened around her and stood, keeping her cradled against his body. "We need to get her out of here."

Tears came, quickly followed by the ugly cry. Wrenching sobs accompanied by an inhuman wail that could only be coming from her from the way Tevin held her closer.

"Vixen's bringing a car," Maddie said.

Cassandra didn't remember Tevin carrying her to the car or the drive back to Broken Peak. She didn't even remember him carrying her through the underground tunnel into the Lodge or when he set her down on the bed.

CHAPTER TWENTY-SIX

TEVIN ignored Maddie's declarations of doctor patient confidentiality and refused to leave Cassie's side.

He had wanted to get her into a bath to wash off the filth left behind from the wizard, but Maddie stopped him from carrying Cassie up to Vixen and Bray's room. She pushed him toward his bedroom.

And now they were at an impasse. He wasn't budging no matter if Maddie glared at him all night. And Cassie hadn't let go of him. He didn't mind her clinging to him as much as he minded why she didn't let go.

His arms tightened around her. Tevin failed Cassie. He swore he would keep her safe, that she wouldn't get hurt. But the swelling on her cheek and bruises on her body disagreed.

Maddie sighed and closed the door. She came over to Cassie and lifted her face to better see the extent of the damage.

Tevin wanted to push her away. He didn't want anyone else touching her. Ever. But that wasn't possible if he wanted to make sure she'd be okay.

Maddie tilted her head back and looked up her nose while brushing her thumb over her cheek. Cassie flinched and Tevin growled.

He wanted to turn away and unsee everything, but he wouldn't let Cassie out of his sight ever again.

The soft sounds coming from Maddie as she examined Cassie annoyed the hell out of Tevin. He didn't want sounds and noises. He wanted words. Assurances that she'd be okay.

"Considering the bruises and swelling, we need to do a sonogram, Cassie."

"The poppy seed?" Cassie asked.

Tevin could hear the tears in her voice.

"Closer to a kidney bean now." Maddie walked to the door and opened it. Peeking her head outside, she spoke quietly with whoever was standing there. A few seconds later, the door opened entirely and Maddie wheeled the machine into the room.

Before either Cassie or Tevin could agree with the decision, Maddie was futzing with the machine.

"Out." Tevin growled.

He needed a few minutes alone with Cassie. Just the two of them. So much needed to be said and their words didn't need an audience.

"Tevin, any delays will limit our options and could add more complications."

He didn't care. They'd take care of the complications after they showed up. Not before.

His wolf agreed.

Only this time when he growled, he intended it as a threat. Maddie might be a friend and Cassie's doctor, but he would fight her if he had to. Whatever she heard or saw was enough, and she left the room and closed the door behind her. The look she gave him before she left told him he needed to be nice to Cassie.

Like she had to worry. Tevin didn't plan on being anything other than nice to her. They just needed to talk. Especially since Maddie and Cassie used code words while speaking about the baby.

Tevin pulled her into his lap and closer to him. She wouldn't be able to pull away from him. Not until they had their talk.

"Cassie?"

She didn't twist away like he expected, but she didn't say anything either. He counted it as a win.

"Cassie, your grandma told me. She didn't mean to, but she didn't know that I didn't know yet."

He either said the wrong thing, and she was taking her time forming an argument, or she was giving him the silent treatment. He didn't like either option.

"Cassie?"

"Did you look for me just because of that?"

"What? Cassie? Baby, what the hell kind of question is that?"

"When I was locked in a room there, all I wanted was for you to come and save me."

The words hit Tevin in the chest, but not in a bad way. He loved that Cassie wanted him to save her. And he loved it even more that he did save her. He didn't love that she needed saving. As he ran his hands through her hair he was reminded that she needed a bath and his need to talk was going to mean she'd have to wait.

Fuck, he was a selfish asshole.

"I wish I'd gotten there sooner."

"Tevin you got there."

"What if we had been even a few minutes later?"

"But you weren't. Tevin you came in at the perfect time."

Yeah. He got there. He got there when the maniac was sitting over her and about to plunge a knife into her. When he found them, his wolf took over and clamped his jaws down on the wizard's neck.

He was sure there would be a lecture later on how stupid he was. That he should have given Alexander time to question the wizard. But neither he nor his wolf was thinking. That was the problem with Cassie. His brain stopped working when he was around her. And worse? He didn't fucking care.

He loved that whenever she was near, all he thought about was her. He loved her.

"I love you, Cassie. And so does my wolf. You're ours. Even if you weren't pregnant, you'd still be ours."

Cassie turned in his arms until she faced him. "I love you too, Tevin. And yes, I am yours. I think I've known that since you showed up at my hotel room."

Tevin winced when he saw the bruises and dried blood on her face. Most of the blood had come from the wizard, but some of it was Cassie's. Seeing it nearly broke him. The last thing she needed was for him to come apart, so he pulled himself together. She needed him steady and stable. He hadn't been able to keep her safe, but he could give her stability.

"Cassie, why didn't you tell me about the baby?"

"You were in the penalty box." She pressed her hands against his chest. "I was going to tell you when you knocked on my door. That's why I went to the bar. But then you did your whole possessive wolf thing. And then I was going to tell you the night when everyone was here figuring out that the man you saw was a wizard. But you decided you knew what was best for me and put me under house arrest."

"Okay, we can deal with that later. But in the future, you don't keep secrets from me. You don't keep things from me. Not *me*. Not *ever*." He kissed her. She whimpered and he felt badly. He didn't like causing her pain, but he needed to kiss her. He needed to feel her. And she understood that.

Cassie pulled back slowly and tried to smile, but couldn't hide the pain.

"And you don't keep things from me. Not ever." She repeated his words back at him.

"Not when it comes to us, I won't." It wasn't what she wanted to hear, but it would have to be enough.

"You're not upset about being a dad? I didn't expect anything from you, but when I first found out, I decided I wanted this baby."

"Cassie, I'm not mad at all. I mean, we were stupid that night. I didn't know you were a witch, but still. The last thing I am is angry and I don't regret any of it."

Tevin hadn't had a lot of time to think about Cassie being pregnant or what it would be like being a dad. Being a parent with her. But in the short time he'd thought about it, no matter what scenario he played out in his mind, they all included Cassie and him and their baby. They might have been stupid, but it was the best kind of stupid.

Cassie kept her hands pressed to his chest. "Swear?"

"Cross my heart." He rested his forehead against hers.

He wanted to kiss her. Hell, he wanted to make love to her. But it wasn't the time or place. He didn't know *when* it would be time. But before he dwelt on thoughts any longer, he needed to get Maddie back in so he could get Cassie her bath.

After they dealt with everything else, he could deal with finding the right time and the right place.

Tevin cleared his throat and smiled. It wasn't enough according to his wolf, but it would have to do until Maddie finished with her examination.

"Maddie!"

The door opened and Maddie slipped back in the room. "I told everyone they'd have to wait in the kitchen. It's going to take a village to keep Sybil out of here for much longer, so we should hurry."

Tevin nodded. He would have done the same thing if he knew everyone had been lurking outside.

Maddie smiled down at Cassie. "I'm not worried about the sonogram, and you shouldn't be either. You haven't had any bleeding and other than some contusions, it looks like your abdomen wasn't the receiving end of most of the trauma. But once we're done with that, I'm going to do the things that will hurt. A lot. There's a chance you'll hate me when we're through."

When Maddie finished, both Cassie and Tevin were still staring at the screen on the machine. All they saw was a small blob inside a bubble. The baby really did look like a kidney bean. His pup was a fucking kidney bean!

"There's his head." Maddie pointed to the larger portion of the bean.

"His?" Tevin would have been happy with either a girl or a boy, but a boy would be amazing. He could teach him how to hunt, and Foster would have another male to roughhouse with. It was perfect.

"Well, no. I mean, maybe. We won't be able to tell for another two months at least, probably longer. And even then, we could be wrong." Maddie glanced at the screen before looking back at Cassie. "What I can say for sure is that right now everything is fine. Just like I said I thought it would be. But, we also need to make arrangements to find you an obstetrician."

Tevin snapped his head away from the screen and stared at Maddie. What did she mean 'find Cassie an obstetrician'? Wasn't Maddie going to be Cassie's doctor? The more he thought about someone else, possibly a man, putting his hands on Cassie, the less he liked the idea of her finding another doctor.

Maddie flipped off the machine and cleaned up Maddie's stomach. Once she finished, she pressed her palms against Cassie's face and pushed her thumb against the swollen cheek.

Cassie yelped from the pain. Tevin and his wolf growled. And Maddie carried on as though nothing had happened.

"It might be an orbital fracture."

Tevin wanted to kill the wizard all over again. Except this time it wouldn't be quick. He'd take his time and use all the tools they found waiting in the warehouse. The wizard deserved a pain filled death that lasted for an eternity.

CHAPTER TWENTY-SEVEN

THE entire pack, except for Maggie, who was playing with Foster and Moose, sat around the large kitchen table. Memaw and Mac were there as well, and so was Alexander.

Everyone was talking at once, offering suggestions, and not listening to what anyone else said. Which Cassandra had discovered was typical for the pack. Until Vixen cleared her throat or spoke or sent out a silent signal to shut up. Then everyone quieted down for several minutes, before repeating the process over again.

Cassandra had no idea how the pack got anything done, but it seemed to work for them. Instead of adding to the chatter, she sat back and observed. She was part of Broken Peak Pack now. And so was her grandma, tangentially at least.

After five more minutes of talking that didn't lead anywhere, Vixen did her throat clearing thing then looked over at Alexander.

"You've been remarkably quiet."

"I deciphered the runes on the table. And I think I can say why we didn't realize any powerful wizards existed before his appearance."

Memaw snorted and rolled her eyes. "Are you going to share it with us, or make us guess?"

"He was killing supernaturals and taking their power. A wizard's power comes from within, they can't tap the magic outside of them like witches do. He must have discovered some writings and learned how to steal magic."

Cassandra flinched and Tevin reached for hand and squeezed her fingers. If Tevin hadn't found her, she would have been dead and the wizard would have had her magic.

"Then the rumors running through the shifter community about Broken Peak Pack would have been a magnet to him." Mac said.

"That's sick." One of the males said.

"Great, just what we need, serial killer wizards running around murdering supernaturals for their magic. Like we don't have enough to deal with already." Bray grumbled and crossed his arms over his chest. "You think he was working alone?"

"Probably. I can't see how he'd work with anyone without killing them. But yeah, like Mac said, Broken Peak and War is the mother lode of magic right now and other supernaturals might be drawn here. It's something we need to watch out for." By using the word we, Alexander informed everyone sitting in the room that he was one of them now. Regardless of their feelings on the matter, he was now part of whatever was in the works. "Vixen. It's time you called up some of the favors owed to you. If shifters are already sending hit squads, the other supernaturals will follow. I'm limited to when I can help and you can't spend the rest of your lives hunkered down at Broken Peak and expect the balance to miraculously be restored. You're going to need friends you can trust."

Vixen cocked her head to the side in a stilted way that made her look more machine than female while she considered Alexander's suggestions. As though finding them satisfactory, she gave him a curt nod then swiveled her head towards Mac.

"With Cassandra here, all the pieces are in place. And as much as it pains me to admit, Alexander is right. It's going to get a lot worse. It's time everyone knows what you are *and* everyone learns just what Broken Peak Pack is now that all the pieces are in place."

Cassandra had only heard about Vixen's griffin and never actually seen her. But from stories the others had shared, Vixen was a killing machine and her griffin considered most everyone outside the pack an enemy that should be destroyed. Supposedly they were working on discriminating friend from foe, but Cassandra wasn't volunteering anytime soon to test that theory.

"What about the hyena?" Tevin asked. "Have we gotten any more info on the pack from the southeast?"

"Narrowing it down. Hopefully with what's happened to their last three hires, they'll think before sending someone else out." Vixen answered.

"I'm still confused about the wizard. Do we know anything about him?" Cassandra finally spoke.

"Not yet, but we're working on it. Once we get an identification, we can look at his contacts and see if we can find any other wizards." Danielle answered. She'd been sitting in front of computers for hours, much to Leighton's frustration, but still hadn't found anything yet. "He was really off the grid. I didn't think it was possible, but he managed it."

"You sound impressed."

"I am. Do you know how hard it is not to have any way to trace you? He had to have been using false identification."

"Probably stole the IDs from the supernaturals he killed."

"I'm not giving up, though." Danielle looked over at Vixen. "Unless you need me for something else, I'm going back to my computers."

Vixen shook her head, but it was Bray who answered. "We'll send someone if we need you."

Both Danielle and Leighton left the kitchen, but the room didn't feel any less crowded.

"With Cassandra being the Witch in the journals, is that it? It feels kind of anticlimactic, like there should have been fireworks or something."

"Fireworks?" Jackson asked his mate.

"Well, not fireworks, but she has magic, maybe a light show or something."

"You missed what she did to the hyena." Mac muttered.

"Just like supernaturals will be attracted to this place, so will the writings. Your job is just beginning, Eleanor. New books will be discovered in some great aunt's trunk, and you'll be the one to examine them. In fact, you can start with the books I packed in Cassandra's bag." Memaw stared at Eleanor with a small smile. Like she could see something in her future, except that couldn't be right since Memaw couldn't read the future and wasn't a clairvoyant.

"You look disappointed, El." Jackson grinned and winked at her. "We're you hoping to get hold of the book I've seen you staring at when you think no one's looking?"

"What? No. I mean, sure, I'd love to, but no."

"You can't read it." Cassandra added.

"Oh, and I would never ask." Eleanor's eyes widened.

"No, I mean, you won't be able to read it. It's keyed to the Voisin women, so unless you're a long-lost relative, you wouldn't be able to see anything except squiggles." Cassandra explained the magic of the book.

"And trust me when I say The Book has a mind of its own sometimes and is more trouble than it's worth." Memaw glared at the old tome. As though it had done her countless wrongs in the past.

"The books are in the trunk of my car." Cassandra answered the question she knew Eleanor was about to ask.

The tiny human hopped to her feet, pulling her mate with her out the kitchen. "Come on, you can help carry them."

Delia, the regal wolf shifter who Cassandra hadn't quite been able to warm up to, looked over at Vixen. "I think it's time we called the Council and my family. It's time for the packs to choose their fates and stand with my brother or alone. Once the wolf shifters move, the other shifters will follow, and we can decide how to handle the holdouts."

"Good idea." Bray stood and pulled Vixen to her feet. As much as Vixen and Bray led the pack together, Vixen had a tendency to take things over. But Bray was good at keeping her in check. Like right now.

Allard, Delia, Vixen, and Bray followed Eleanor and Jackson out the room and down the hall to the left.

"I can see where this is headed." Finley looked around the room. "Before you say anything. I'm off to find Maggie, and to make sure she and Foster haven't done something weird with Moose."

And then it was just Tevin, Cassandra, Memaw, Mac, and Alexander in the room.

It was like everything had been planned ahead so only they would be left. Cassandra didn't think it was anyone's doing, but maybe magic intervened on their behalf.

Once everything was quiet and those in the kitchen were sure no one was lingering close to the doorway, Memaw took a deep breath.

Great. It was either going to be a lecture, or she was about to drop something that Cassandra was sure she didn't want to hear.

"Alexander. Have you ever known of any supernaturals successfully getting pregnant."

The vampire, as Cassandra had recently learned what he was, stared at both her and Tevin. "Never. They've paired up, but never had a child."

"We know children of shifters and humans are latents." Mac added.

"Wait." Tevin blurted out. "What's wrong with the baby?"

"Nothing. This is just uncharted territory." Alexander reassured him.

"Nothing in The Book, Memaw?"

"No. It's being remarkably quiet." She glared at the leather cover. "Too quiet if you ask me."

"So, our baby could be a latent then?"

Alexander slowly shook his head. "It's not that mixed pairings didn't have children, Cassandra. They couldn't. And none of the shifters knew you were pregnant. Didn't anyone stop to question why?"

"I've been ignoring the question for as long as possible." Mac stared across the room at the wall.

Tevin was losing his patience. "So what are you all trying to say then? Because I can't figure it out and Cassie looks as confused as I'm feeling."

"We won't know until the baby's born, or we're lucky and find some lost writings that will explain it, but your baby will have access to both moon and earth magic." Alexander said. "That will be a lot of magic in one creature. More than that wizard managed to steal."

"Nothing will happen to our baby." Tevin growled and pulled Cassandra into his lap.

She let him because she understood the anxiety he and his wolf were feeling. The same anxiety coursed through her. If Cassandra was a target just for being a witch, every supernatural with the slightest desire for power would be after their child.

"Go on. Get out of here, you two. I'm sure you have a lot of things you'd rather be doing than sitting here listening to us prattle on." Memaw sighed and waved them away with a brush of her hand.

Tevin took the suggestion like it was an order. He stood and carried Cassandra to their room before someone found something for them to do.

CHAPTER TWENTY-EIGHT

CASSANDRA stepped out of the shower and stood in front of the mirror. Most of the swelling on her face had gone down and the bruises had turned to an ugly shade of yellow.

Vixen had been true to her word and started construction on the cabins. The first cabin had been built in record time and Tevin had claimed it before anyone else, using the pregnancy card to get priority.

They'd just moved into the two bedroom house with its own small kitchen and living area. Perfect for a small family. And Tevin promised her they would add more rooms when they had more children. One for each baby. Cassandra was frightened to ask just how many rooms he planned on adding.

It had been two weeks since Tevin saved her from the wizard, and he still hadn't touched her.

He kissed her and held her, but nothing more.

The house arrest had been lifted, but he still wouldn't let her outside of the cabin or the Lodge without someone else with her. She had gotten closer to the other females in the pack though and didn't mind spending time with them when Tevin was out on patrol.

But it was Delia she found herself spending the most time with. The female was aloof, but once Cassandra learned her background, she understood it. They spoke about everything. From the baby to the political maneuvering the shifters were doing and what the other supernaturals might do.

It was also Delia who explained why Tevin was acting like Cassandra would break with the slightest gust of wind. Even though everything that happened with the wizard happened to Cassandra, it also happened to Tevin. He was standing in a field filled with unknowns and didn't know how to respond or if he should respond.

Tevin blamed himself. And so did Cassandra, at first. But from talking with Delia and Maddie, Cassandra realized that even though she stepped outside the Lodge, the wizard was the one waiting. She couldn't control the wizard, any more than she could control whether the sun rose or set.

However, she could control her response. Delia recommended a therapist, someone her family used in Chicago. They'd been speaking on the phone every day and it helped. During the last conversation, Tevin had sat outside the cabin on its small porch, giving her privacy while she spent the entire time talking about his unwillingness to touch her.

The therapist told her to take control. That she needed to show Tevin that she was all right and not just tell him.

Cassandra knew they had the rest of the day to themselves. Tevin didn't have any patrols. No meetings had been planned. And everyone was off doing their own thing, taking advantage of the respite.

It was the perfect time for Cassandra to take the therapist's advice.

She placed her hands over her breasts with her little fingers barely touching over her sternum. The boob fairy had arrived and Cassandra had a brand-new pair of boobs. Tevin needed to appreciate them. She lifted her chin at her reflection, daring the image to disagree.

Beneath the faded bruises, she was still the same Cassandra she'd always been. She just needed Tevin to believe that too.

Her hands slid down to her stomach. She pressed her fingers against the slight pooch she noticed the night before and smiled.

Despite everything that had happened, She wouldn't change one thing. Not even if someone offered her the world. Tevin was a good male. She just needed to remind him and his wolf that he was.

She combed the tangles from her hair and wondered if maybe a haircut would help. Maybe shorter? She'd have to remember to ask Delia what she thought.

Standing in front of the mirror wasn't getting her closer to her goal. With a deep breath, she pushed her hair behind her ears and walked into the bedroom. She found the pale green shirt Tevin had worn that night hanging in the closet and pulled it on. She loved wearing his clothes. It was like his arms were always around her, even when he wasn't there.

She went to the Bluetooth speaker and connected her phone. After looking through the different songs, she selected *In His Arms*.

The raw sound of the song came from the speaker, filling the silent room. She wrapped her arms around her chest and swayed around the room to the song.

Cassandra closed her eyes and imagined that night at the Dirty Whistle. They existed together only for that moment and nothing else mattered. Just two people who found each other.

She turned and swayed and found Tevin watching her from the door of the bedroom.

"Tevin." She smiled.

He pushed off the wall and returned her smile. "I heard music, but I'll leave you alone."

"Wait."

"I don't want to interrupt."

"I don't want you to go."

Tevin opened his mouth, but closed it before saying anything.

"Dance with me?"

She wanted him closer to her, but he stepped away. The next song on the playlist started, an upbeat Ed Sheeran song, and while fun to listen to, not the greatest choice for a seduction. But she couldn't change it without Tevin running away as soon as she turned her back.

"Please?" She held her arm out to him.

He took one step. Then another. "Really?"

"Yes."

Another step. "You're sure?"

"More than I am that I'm yours and you're mine."

Two more steps and he stood closer to her. Not as close as she would have liked, but it was a start. His hands held her waist as they swayed to the music, which had thankfully changed to *What We Ain't Got.*

Cassandra lifted her head and looked at him. He was still the same handsome male he'd been that first night.

"I missed you."

"I try to spend as much time with you as I can, but I have to do patrols."

"Tevin, that's not what I meant. I meant I miss you. You don't look at me the way you used to. Or touch me."

He looked down and she watched as he struggled with a response. Did he tell her what he thought, even if it hurt her? Or did he not say anything?

Before he found an excuse to run away, she wrapped her arms around his neck and rested her head on his shoulder. "You made me a promise once."

"Yeah, and what happened? You got hurt." He kissed the top of her head.

"But you weren't the one who hurt me."

"You still got hurt. If something happened to you, I would have died. Cassie, I can't lose you. Even thinking about what might have happened is enough to make both me and my wolf panic."

"I'm still here. And what might have happened didn't. But that wasn't the promise I was thinking about."

Tevin stroked the back of his fingers over her faded bruise. "I hate that he marked you. It's my job to keep you safe and I failed. How the hell am I supposed to keep our baby safe?"

Cassandra laughed. She couldn't help it. For the past weeks she'd been worried that Tevin was worried about her, but it was about their baby. She understood it. She had the same irrational fears when she realized that soon there would be a tiny creature totally dependent on her for everything. She had been convinced that when it came to mothers, she would be at the top of the list of the worst mothers in the world.

"Well, you don't keep them safe." That's what her grandma told her. "We'll have our share of cuts and bruises and if we're unlucky, broken bones. But you figure it out as you go."

His hand skimmed along her back and arm to her hand. He wove his fingers through hers and squeezed. "I'm supposed to keep him safe."

She brought their hands up between them, between their hearts. "And you'll be great at it. But babies and kids get hurt. That's what they do. Then they get better and get hurt again."

"Why do you think our kid will have so many accidents?"

"Because they do. Look at Foster. Just the other day he got his head caught between the spindles on the front porch. Kids are ticking time bombs, finding everything that might kill them and playing with it. Delia told me about a pup in her pack who put a fork in an outlet. When Delia asked her why she did it, the girl said it fit. By the way, she's still alive. Even though Delia wanted to kill her."

Tevin's embrace tightened and he pulled her closer, pressing their hands between them.

"You're okay, Cassie?" He led them to the bed and pulled her down next to him. "You had to talk with someone about what happened."

She slid closer to him, nestling her body against his. "I don't think anyone is okay."

"That's not an answer." His arm came around her and his head rested on hers.

"And you avoid all my questions. But yeah, I'm all right. I swear. I'm talking to the therapist because I was worried about us, not because of me."

"You're worried about us?" Tevin pulled away, but Cassandra had wrapped her arms and legs around him, making it difficult for him to move.

"Of course I am."

"There's an us?"

"Tevin, do you listen to what you say? Because I thought we settled there being an us weeks ago. And then replayed it again a few days later." As much as the male frustrated her, she loved that he seemed genuinely shocked that she accepted there was an us.

He grinned and looked over at her. "Well, you pretty much say the opposite of whatever I say. So I wasn't sure."

Cassandra took a breath. "I don't blame you for anything, Tevin."

Tevin didn't say anything. Instead, he pulled her closer, squeezing her tight.

She slid down from the bed and knelt between his legs. Tevin's eyes widened, and he placed his hands on his legs, like he didn't know what else to do with them.

She unbuttoned her shirt, watching him the entire time. His gaze never left her face. She slid the shirt off and dropped it to the floor.

"Cassie..."

"Yeah?"

Tevin swallowed hard. His gaze roamed down her body. She licked her dry lips and he groaned.

He lifted his hand, but before he touched her, he pulled it back.

Nope. He wasn't going to get to play the hesitant game. It was time for Cassandra to take control. She took his hands and placed them on her breasts. "Still me."

"Still you."

She moved his hands down to her stomach. "And this right here, Tevin. This is us. And this is the reason we will always make sure that us is okay."

The weeks since Tevin had touched her had been just as hard on him as they had been on her. His hands slid to her hips, and he pulled her closer to him.

"Cassie, are you okay?" His unblinking gaze never left her eyes as he waited for her answer.

She pressed closer, standing right between his legs and against the bed. "I'm okay, Tevin."

They leaned towards each other, meeting halfway as their lips pressed together. His hands moved up her body, cradling her cheeks as his tongue pushed between her lips.

His touch held gentleness and love and reverence. The devotion made her eyes water.

He pulled his face back and wiped away the tears with his thumbs. "I don't think I am though."

"You will be." She wrapped her arms around his neck and held him to her. "I need you, Tevin."

Tevin pulled her into his lap. His hands drew large circles over her back, soothing them both. Cassandra dropped her arm and rested her hand on his hip. She moved her hand further up when he didn't pull away from the touch.

With a swift movement, Tevin spun her around so her back was to his chest and his erection pressed against her through his pants. She held still, allowing him to direct everything.

His lips traced the spot between her neck and shoulder. When he bit down gently on the flesh, she closed her eyes and held her breath. Was he finally going to mark her? To claim her?

"I will always need you, Cassie."

Two weeks of not having the touch from the male she wanted had been an eternity. They might have been together, but she had still been alone. Two weeks was a long time to be alone.

Tevin lifted her up and laid her back on the bed. He bent down and kissed her before his lips found another place to kiss. The underside of her breasts. Her stomach. Her hips. The spot where her leg joined her body.

Her nipples stiffened in anticipation of his touch and her hips lifted towards him. Tevin grinned as he looked up at her before returning his mouth to the inside of her thigh. Her head fell back against the pillows, and she gripped the comforter in her hands. He nipped at the skin before moving on to his target.

The tip of his tongue ran the length of her pussy. Her body writhed beneath him as he pressed down her hips. As his tongue swept back down, he pushed it into her entrance before he pulled away and wrapped his lips around her clit. She pulled her legs up, bending her knees with her feet flat on the bed and pounded her hands against the bed. Even if he held her hips in place, the rest of her body could move and she opened herself up to him.

Tevin pulled away and moved up her body. Gone was the grace and prowess he usually possessed. In its place was the fumbling of a teenager. He barely managed to pull his cock from his pants without falling off the bed.

The head of his cock pressed against her entrance, and she closed her eyes, wanting more from him. "Make love to me, Tevin."

He kissed her, teasing her lips and tongue with licks and nips. She wrapped her arms around his broad shoulders and her legs around his waist, pulling him deeper into her as her lips lifted.

Tevin took his time, moving slowly with long deliberate strokes. His hands pressed down above her shoulders, and he gazed into her eyes. "I will always make love to you, Cassie."

Their movements matched the beat of the song playing. Slow and languid. They took their time. Hips moving together as one while they looked into each other's eyes. It couldn't last. They knew that. Two weeks was too long to be apart. But there would be more later. After they rested, they could take their time relearning everything.

She arched her back and tightened her muscles around his cock buried deep inside her. Tevin growled, but didn't look away. He kissed his way to her neck, delivering teasing bites to her skin.

Cassandra moaned and the involuntary contractions around his cock along with the flood of her wetness, carried him over the edge with her. With a hard thrust, he released inside her and bit down hard on her neck. Breaking the skin.

Screaming out in pleasure, she locked her ankles around his back, holding him tight against her body.

Tevin lifted his body up and off her, but she stopped him.

"Stay."

"I'm too heavy. I'll hurt you."

"You can never hurt me, Tevin."

He dropped his mouth to her neck and licked at the bite mark. She dragged her fingers across his back, tickling his skin, wishing she could ease the pain and hurt he carried.

"You can't hurt me, Tevin. You're not capable of hurting me." She whispered in his ear, reminding both of them.

"You're mine."

"I'm yours. And you're mine."

TURN THE PAGE FOR *BROKEN WITCH* EXTRAS, INCLUDING

The official, Jules Crisare-Sanctioned "What Kind of Shifter are You?" Quiz

An excerpt from the The Sentinels of the Silver Orb novel, *DESTINED HEIR*

And More!

THE OFFICIAL "WHAT KIND OF SHIFTER ARE YOU?" QUIZ

You've read Broken Hero and laughed at the antics of the Broken Peak Pack and cheered when Bray claimed Vixen and accidentally on purpose released the Griffin lurking inside of her. Right? I mean maybe you didn't do all those things, but let's just pretend you have. Now, I bet you're wondering where you'd fit in the pack. Would you be a wolf shifter? Or a griffin shifter? Or maybe another kind of shifter entirely. Well, you no longer have to wonder. In the short time it takes you to answer the questions below, you'll find out what kind of shifter you are.

WHAT SHIFTER AM I?

(If you want to find out what kind of shifter your partner is, replace "you" with "he/she/they". Depending on the result, you might want to keep it to yourself.)

1. When Vixen and Bray invite you to a barbecue at Broken Peak, you:

    a. Hide in the woods and hope no one finds you

    b. Show up earlier and be the last to leave and drink the most moonshine

2. Vixen asks you to steal a shifter artifact from a private collector who refuses to sell (there's no chance of getting caught), you:

    a. Tell her no way

    b. Tell her sure, why not

3. Vixen thinks you should find a mate, you:

    a. Go out with whoever Mac recommends, and of course they're a perfect match, so you agree.

    b. Create profiles on shifter-r-us with the rest of Broken Peak Pack and go out on group dates so your friends can give you instant advice. Plus, if they don't like your friends, they aren't for you.

4. War passed a new ordinance, barring all concealed weapons, even daggers, you:

> a. Don't bring the dagger Vixen got for you into town and leave it at home instead

> b. Ignore the ordinance, besides it's not like you go to War all that often

5. After a long day chasing down false alarms that led no where followed by a double dose of training from Vixen, you just want to go home and fall into bed, but your best friend sends a text, asking if you want to go out for dinner in thirty minutes, you:

> a. Call them back right away, since you plan on venting and your best friend is a great listener

> b. Ignore the message and call your friend back the next morning, you plan on spending the night alone with your favorite book

6. While walking through the park late at night with no one around, you see a new "Keep Off Grass" sign, you:

> a. Complain to yourself, but avoid walking on the grass

> b. Yank the sign out, throw it into the trees, then gleefully hop around on the grass since there's no more sign to stop you

ANSWERS

1. a=1, b=0

3. a=0, b=1

4. a=1, b=0

5. a=0, b=1

6. a=1, b=0

Add up your points! Have the number? Great, now if you scored:

0-1 GRIFFIN
Always up for a group hunt or hanging out with the pack, even if it means exploring forbidden territory.

2 WOLF
You take every opportunity to spend time with your friend and pack and always obey your Alpha.

3-4 COYOTE
You don't mind occasionally hanging out with friends, but prefer to spend most of your time alone with your still and never let something like rules get in the way of doing something.

5-6 BEAR
You're the strong and silent type, always ready to help your few close friends you have as long as your aren't breaking any rules.

AN EXCERPT FROM THE SENTINELS OF THE SILVER ORB NOVEL, *DESTINED HEIR*

Lennon Lyall has known Geneva Caine since she was in grade school. Geneva is smart, beautiful, and completely out of bounds. Not because she's his sister's best friend, but because she's not entirely what she seems. Geneva has crushed on Lennon since she was thirteen years old and had her first boyfriend. She never thought Lennon would ever see her as anything more than his younger sister's annoying friend. But after learning about shifters, she agrees to work for Lennon in the family business. She doesn't expect to fall in love with her childhood crush or to give it all up so Lennon can become the Alpha his pack needs.

GENEVA SAT AT THE TABLE in the dark corner of the resort's restaurant and stared at Lennon. Of course, he chose a luxury resort to stay at instead of a hotel off the side of the highway. She was almost certain he paid the staff to keep the restaurant open since it was just the two of them in the massive room filled with empty tables. It wasn't like the Lyalls couldn't afford the payoff, but something about the sentiment bothered her. Her emotions confused her, but she didn't want to unravel the mess, which all began in the morning with a knock at the door.

She picked at her pasta. Geneva wasn't hungry, and the conversation had done nothing to improve her appetite, but Lennon insisted she order something. Delia had stayed in the suite with Molly — Lennon had stopped and bought the kid a happy meal and Geneva had been jealous. She craved a greasy burger and fries and had suggested as much to Lennon, but he ignored her.

She peered into the dining room, taking in the luxe decor and staff who hovered well within sight, but not too close. Geneva and Lennon must have looked like they were about to break up, or he was about to propose to her. Why else would he insist the dining room stay open? The former would imply they had a relationship. And she had imagined the latter when she was at junior high. Geneva used to dream about marrying Lennon Lyall when she was thirteen, and he was a cute teenager in high school, who drove an expensive car. The trifecta of tween fantasies. Not that Geneva still had those tween fantasies, but there was something about Lennon that made her want him to want her.

"You know things will change right, Geneva?" He watched her, waiting for her answer. No matter her response, her future was going to change. Dramatically. She witnessed her friend and two others turn into wolves. There wasn't much else that belonged on a list of things that qualified as more dramatic.

Geneva pushed a piece of pasta around her plate with her fork and ignored his question. He had spent the past hour trying to convince her it was all going to be okay, but different.

Lennon sighed, then finished his wine in a few gulps before refilling his glass. "You can't give me the silent treatment forever, Neva."

She gazed at him. He wasn't the same man she assumed he was earlier that morning, but her heart still pounded against her ribs when he was close. Every time he looked at her, the world stopped on its axis, and she was the only woman in the world. "Why not? Delia's been doing that to me. For over fifteen years. Why are you talking to me and not her?"

"She was told not to tell you." Lennon gazed at the base of his wine glass. Like the admission embarrassed him.

"By you?"

"No. Our father. He asked me to talk with you instead." Lennon reached out across the table, but stopped himself from taking her hand. "You probably have a lot of questions."

Geneva snatched the glass of wine off the table, mindless of the deep red liquid splashing near the rim. "That's the understatement of my lifetime."

His toe brushed against hers under the table. "I'm sorry, Neva. If I could stop you from finding out, I would."

"Why?" She tilted her head back to better see him. She wanted to know why he thought she didn't deserve to be in this tremendous secret of theirs. It wasn't the finding out her best friend was a myth that hurt. It was her best friend not telling her that caused the hurt.

"I feel like a broken record." He lowered his voice and leaned across the table. Lennon pulled the glass from her and wrapped his hand around her fingers. "This changes things. A lot. Your life won't be the same anymore."

Geneva lowered her gaze to their linked hands. The gesture intended to comfort her, but she wished — for a moment — he wanted to hold her hands just because. "How?" She was on a roll with the one-word questions.

"I can't say how for sure yet. Dad will have some ideas, but he hasn't shared them with me."

"Give me the cliff notes version."

Lennon inhaled and rubbed small circles across the back of her hand with his thumb. "I'm not sure there is one. No matter how I explain it to you, it will take time."

Geneva focused on his thumb as it slid along her skin. "So, I'm not going crazy?"

His hand twitched, but he didn't pull away from her. Lennon held on. "No. I told you already. You aren't crazy. You are as sane as you were yesterday."

Geneva blinked and sucked in a lungful of oxygen. She might as well jump into with both feet. "What happens next?" She stared right into Lennon's eyes.

"We go back to Chicago. Dad decides what to do with you. Then we figure out how you'll fit in with the Pack."

Geneva's forehead wrinkled at the word Pack. She ignored the part about her fitting into it. Or at least tried to. She squeaked out the offending word. "Pack?"

Lennon stood from the table and grabbed the bottle of wine. He pulled her next to him and smiled. "Let's take a walk."

She looked at her nearly full plate. It wasn't as if she was going to eat the rest of her dinner.

Lennon led her through the tables and out the restaurant. Without looking at her, he guided Geneva across the vacant lobby and out into the gardens in back. The out-of-the-way resort wasn't even close to a small town. It was in the middle of nowhere with none of the sounds found in a city.

She smiled, "why Chicago?"

Lennon pulled on her hand until they walked side by side along the gravel path through the flowers. "Because it's the central location of our Pack."

"But it's a city?"

Lennon lowered his head and grinned at her. "A city with a lot of parks and Mom and Dad don't live in the city. They live in the suburbs."

"But you live in the city." Geneva almost stumbled over her feet. His gaze, no matter what they might have been talking about, sent her stomach into a flood of nerves. He no longer saw his sister's best friend. She liked his look. She wanted more of that look. Even if it accompanied pointy teeth and a shedding problem.

"Yeah. And there are plenty of parks around me. I don't spend all my time in the city, Neva."

They walked closer to the woods, and Lennon drank from the bottle. If she bothered to consider the moment, she would have recognized her happiness from being with him. Regardless of everything else that happened during the day, she enjoyed being with Lennon. It could have been the end of the world, and she would have been happy.

Lennon stopped and pulled her against him, wrapping an arm around her waist like he did when Mark interrupted their getaway. He bent his head. He was going to kiss her. She wanted him to kiss her. Desperately. Instead, he lowered his head to her neck and inhaled.

If Geneva made a list of the ten sexiest things that had happened to her, what Lennon did right then would have made number one. His breath danced across her skin. She listened to his deep inhale and imagined he smelled more than her perfume. At least she assumed he did. Geneva closed her eyes. His lips millimeters away from her neck. The slightest movement by either of them meant his lips would be on her skin.

"I can smell him on you." Lennon set the bottle on the grass.

Geneva's eyes snapped open, and she stepped back. His arm held her tight, so she didn't move far. "What?"

"I can smell your boyfriend."

"Ex."

"If I can smell him on you, he's not an ex." Lennon growled low.

He didn't aim his anger at her. At least she hoped he didn't. "What do you mean?

Lennon wrapped his other arm around her and pulled her flush against his chest. "I mean he left his scent all over you. Deliberately."

With each deep breath, his nose brushed against her hair. He smelled her hair. If anyone else had done it, it would have been creepy.

But coming from Lennon, it was kind of hot. "I haven't seen him in two weeks. I've taken a few showers in the meantime."

"I don't know what he is, Geneva, you need to avoid him." His hand stroked the length of her back.

Geneva tilted her head back and looked at him. "Until he showed up tonight, I hadn't seen him since I broke up with him. I promise."

Lennon stared at her. She wondered if he would kiss her. Geneva didn't understand his frustration or annoyance with Mark. She didn't understand why Lennon turned possessive. Before that day, she hadn't been more than an afterthought to him. On holidays or vacations, Lennon only included her because she was there with Delia.

She closed her eyes and breathed. What was the worst that would happen, right? She reached up on her toes and pressed her lips against his. Before Lennon rejected her, she stepped away. Or tried to step away. Lennon kept his arms around her. He refused to let her get away from him.

Lennon breathed in deeply again and a warm flush moved across Geneva's cheeks. Lennon's thumb moved up and down over the small of her back, and she focused on his touch. If he touched her, it meant he wasn't upset she kissed him. Right?

"You will ignore Mark." His voice rumbled through his chest and Geneva giggled from the way his muscles vibrated against her.

She focused on that instead of the command issued by her best friend's brother. The man she kissed. She liked Lennon. Like liked like, and sure he was being nice to her, but she held no delusions of Lennon ever pursuing a relationship with her. Since he wasn't pursuing a relationship, he didn't have a right to dictate who she talked to or with.

"He won't call. He was already chatting with some girls planning on attending grad school in New York." Geneva liked that she didn't agree to obey him as much as she gave him information he could find satisfying.

"I don't care, Neva." His hands tangled into her ponytail, and he pulled her head back, so he could look into her eyes. "If he calls you, or emails you, or even shows up at your door, you ignore him." He kept her head still without hurting her and shifted closer to her, almost brushing his lips against hers. "You don't pick up his calls, let them go to voice mail, and if he emails you, delete them."

Geneva saw the flash of yellow in his eyes again and almost flinched. It took all her self-control not to jerk away from him and run to their room. Well, her self-control and the fact she was positive Delia was a werewolf-person-woman thing. She assumed Lennon was one as well, but not the woman part.

"If he shows up at your door, you call me, Neva." His lips brushed against hers. Too light to be anything but an accident, and Geneva groaned. "Promise me."

Geneva nodded her head. She wanted to feel Lennon's lips against hers again and hoped he might reward her if she complied with his demands. Lennon's reward was better than any brief touch of lips against lips.

He moved his hand from her back to the side of her face and rubbed his thumb against her cheek. Geneva leaned into his hand and closed her eyes. With his other hand holding her head still, she couldn't move far. But he could.

Lennon leaned down and pressed his lips against hers. His lips crushed against hers. His tongue pushed against her mouth, demanding entry, and she parted her lips. Teeth nipped at her tongue and lips. Demanding obedience. He controlled her movements and the ferocity of the kiss. He controlled everything. She closed her eyes and breathed into the kiss. She tried to lean against him, but his hands kept her in the position he wanted.

Geneva arched her neck closer to him, but Lennon pulled away, chuckling at her in his usual self-satisfied manner. Geneva didn't know what she wanted to smack him for more. Stopping the kiss or his smug laughter.

Lennon leaned down, brushing his whiskered stubble against her cheek. He pulled away, but kept his hand in her hair, holding. "Neva." The way he spoke her name sent a shot of warmth right to her core. She felt herself growing wet and shifted her hips. The realization made her slightly uncomfortable. "I should have asked for two rooms." He tightened his hand in her hair and this time, when he kissed her, he released whatever control he kept during the first kiss.

His teeth nipped her lips. He sucked her lip between his teeth and pulled at her until Geneva took a few tentative steps closer to him. Lennon pulled her head back and dragged his tongue along her jaw to her ear. He bit at her earlobe, another reminder of the intensity of his arousal. She heard him breathe in and closed her eyes.

"You need to shower, Neva." Lennon growled into her ear. "I can smell him all over you. I never want to smell him on you again." Another nip at her ear. Another reminder he expected her obedience.

Geneva wasn't sure how to respond. His demands warred with her wants and existence as an independent woman. She returned his stare, and his gaze bored into her. Lennon breathe her in, and she shuddered at the intimacy of the act. She saw the way his jaw trembled, the way he walked a line between being the man she remembered and knew so well and the... Geneva didn't have a word for it. Was it a wolf? Or was it something more like a caveman? The more she thought about it, the more she realized she didn't care what it was. She liked something about it. A lot.

She inhaled and exhaled slow even breaths, then opened her mouth to speak. "All right."

Lennon pounced. His mouth found hers, and his tongue forced its way past the seam of her lips. She whimpered, but didn't pull away. His fingers pressed into her shoulders and neck, pulling her closer as he groaned against her mouth.

Geneva wasn't one hundred percent certain, but she heard the word mine between his groans.

WARNING: UNDER THE INFLUENCE OF PREGNANCY
A SILVER SENTINEL SHORT STORY

Cassie stood in front of Tevin in a too tight black dress that showed off the little swell of her belly. They had finally made it past the first trimester and Cassie announced that they could now officially announce the pregnancy. Although, everyone in the Pack already knew, and even everyone who had come to the territory since Cassie's arrival knew.

Cassie's grandma had found more reasons to come and visit and after she got over the fact that Tevin knocked her grand daughter up, she came around to being a great-grandma.

"You look amazing, baby." He wasn't lying. She was still the gorgeous woman he first saw at the Dirty Whistle nearly four months ago. But even better.

Cassie pressed her hands against her stomach and looked at him. Tevin knew what was coming next. Cassie had turned into a gas machine. If It wasn't coming out of one end, it was coming out the other. And since Tevin had a dick, he found it funny. So did Finley. Whenever she got that look on her face, Finley grabbed her finger and pulled. Cassie wasn't nearly as amused as the rest of them.

Tevin glanced down at her feet and the pair of fleece-line boots she was wearing. "Cassie?"

As though on cue, a loud burp answered. Cassie blushed and hid her mouth behind her hand. "What?"

"Why boots?"

"What boots?" She looked down. "Crap. I swear I have no memory of putting them on, Tevin."

He got off the bed and walked to the closet where he found a pair of shoes he bought when they had gone shopping. At some point in the last week, Cassie turned into the female version of Foster. They'd actually started pinning notes to her, so she wouldn't forget things.

Maddie had warned Tevin that pregnancy brain was a real thing, and she would lose brain cells. She told him that Cassie wasn't brain-damaged or anything like that, and if he had any instinct for self-preservation, he wouldn't say a word about it. But he didn't feel okay about it until her grandma confirmed that it was to be expected and Cassie would be back to normal once the baby came out.

Tevin switched over her shoes, mostly because he didn't trust her to get both on before her brain went on another one of its vacations.

"Do we really have to go? Can't you go and leave me here? Tell them that with the morning sickness, I couldn't go?"

"You never had morning sickness."

"They don't know that."

"Cassie, all the mates are going and you made Mac invite your grandma so you won't be all alone. And Delia's parents will be there." Tevin went in for the kill. "Allard even made sure they'd have cronuts."

Cassie perked up at the mention of the word cronuts. They had to send someone into town every day now to get them because she couldn't live without them. Cassie craved cronuts to the point where

Tevin was worried their pup was going to have an addiction when he was finally born.

They still didn't know if they were having a boy or a girl, but like Cassie, he hated using the word it and hated using the words that described the size of the baby even more. Unlike Cassie, he refused to use the word peach, or as she had informed him yesterday, orange.

"I can barely remember my name, how am I going to remember everyone else's?"

"Don't worry about it." He wasn't letting her get out of going, and she knew it. Not only was it time to announce to the rest of the supernatural world that Cassie was pregnant, it was also time everyone knew she was his. Not that they hadn't figured it out already after he ripped out that wizard's throat, but this was official.

Tevin set Cassie down on the bed and kissed her forehead before walking over to the dresser. In the top drawer, under his socks and underwear, sat a jewelry box. And inside the box was a necklace with a pendant formed from two circles. The outer circle had diamonds on both side, but the inside circle had diamonds on one side and sapphires on the other.

He bought it for her months ago. Before he even knew she was pregnant. The blue of the sapphires reminded him of the color of her eyes and even though she already wore a ring, he was trying to bring in the human traditions, he wanted to give her something without having a reason to.

Tevin brought the box back to Cassie and set it in her hands. For a moment he thought he would have to help her open it, but she managed to lift the lid on her own.

The look on her face and the soft gasp of surprise was enough for him to know he did well.

"Why? What's this for?"

"Does there need to be a reason?" He took the box from her hand and pulled the necklace out to fasten it around her neck. From the crinkles that formed in the corners of her eyes, Tevin could tell that she thought he did need a reason. "I got it a while ago and just never found a good reason to give it to you."

"Are you bribing me?"

"Not with the necklace. I'm using cronuts for that."

"Yeah, I am kinda a slut for a cronut."

Tevin pulled her to her feet and pressed his lips against hers. Sure, she was wearing lipstick and her face and hair was all done, but he wanted to kiss his mate. Besides, it wasn't like she'd remember that she put on her makeup. He swore, a goldfish had a better memory than Cassie.

"Ready?" He stepped away from her, but held on to her hands, so she couldn't bolt.

"Do I have a choice."

"Careful, Cassie, I'm keeping track and once you have our baby, you are going over my knee."

He swore his mate flushed at his words. And he knew that look on her face well enough to know that if he didn't get them out the door soon, they'd be undressed. Hell, fuck getting her out of the bedroom, he had to get her out of the cabin. His packmates had almost walked in on them more times than he cared to count. And Finley *had* actually walked in on them once.

Ever since, Finley made a big deal about making a lot of noise before coming into the cabin.

He took her hand and led her from the bedroom towards the door. "Come on, mate, Finley and Maggie are waiting for us."

"But are you sure I just don't look fat?"

"Cassie, you're gorgeous and you look amazing. You look pregnant and not fat. And that dress Maddie got for you is perfect. Real nice." It was too. Maddie recommended the store, and after he compared what Cassie was wearing to what the women who were pregnant in War wore, he decided Cassie was only going to shop there.

They finally made it out of the cabin and down to the garage, but not before Cassie remembered that she forgot her purse, phone, vitamins, and her bag of saltines, just in case morning sickness finally kicked in. Unfortunately, she remembered each item at different times, so it took them almost an hour just to get into the car.

Tevin decided that when it came closer to actually having the baby, he was going to be in charge of getting them to the hospital, or they'd be at risk of having the baby in the tunnel from the Lodge to the garage.

To Finley and Maggie's credit, they didn't roll their eyes once. Tevin rolled his eyes. Twice.

As soon as they stepped into the party, Cassie's worries slid away. The shifters from Delia's pack who had made the trip loved her.

Mac and Sybil had already been there for almost an hour and Cassie latched on to her grandma before venturing into the world of gossiping female shifters who all talked loudly except when they thought something was too horrible to say aloud. In which case, they whispered the word loudly instead. Like it actually made a difference.

"I was worried you weren't going to make it." Mac stepped next to Finley and handed him a drink.

"It was a strong possibility. We had to make four trips back to the cabin before Cassie remembered she forgot something else."

"Vixen was wondering when you were going to show up. She wants to show Cassandra off."

He didn't know how he felt about that. "I'm not sure that's smart, at least not until after she's had the baby."

"No, but it doesn't mean she can't correct some of mistaken beliefs shifters have about the prophecies." Mac took a long drink. "She handle the meeting with the Council okay?"

"Honestly, she kept on bringing up pregnancy brain and I guess one of the councilor's daughters just had a baby and totally got it. He gave me a sympathetic look and ended the meeting."

"They didn't question anything about Alexander's role in finding the wizard?"

"From what I can tell, being pregnant is like a get out of jail free card and it can be used over and over again." Tevin looked around the room until he found Cassie sitting with the mates of Broken Peak, Sybil, Delia's mother, and Geneva. She had a plate full of desserts on the table in front of her.

He watched Vixen move across the floor towards the women. She ignored anyone who tried to speak with her and sat down at the table with the other women.

"Mac?"

"Yeah?"

"What did Maddie tell Vixen that day?" He already thought he knew, but he needed to hear it.

"Maddie told her you found your mate and once you pulled your head out of your ass and figured it out, she'd always come first. Then I told Vixen not to put you in a position where you had to make a choice between pack and Cassandra, because you'd always choose your mate."

Tevin turned and stared at Mac. He hadn't known the old shifter had said anything.

"Maddie might have also told Vixen Cassie was pregnant and you didn't know yet." Mac lifted his glass. "Speaking of which, she's not human, but she comes from a human world. You going to make an honest woman of her so Sybil can stop worrying about it?"

"I did that engagement thing." Tevin sipped his drink and watched his mate from across the room.

"You look at her the same way Bray looks at Vixen."

Tevin smiled and nodded, but didn't look away from Cassie. Someday he might be leading a pack and Cassie would be right by his side. Just like Vixen was right by Bray's side. Their pups would be grown up and Cassie would hold court and keep the pack in line, just like Vixen.

Mac was right. He needed to have an official ceremony. Just like Allard and Delia got.

"After we're done here and everyone's back at Broken Peak, can you make it official? Our mating I mean."

"When?"

"Right afterwards. No one's going to bed until they see us get mated.

"She's going to punish you, you know?"

"Yeah, but I'm counting on her forgetting that she's supposed to be punishing me once I officially make her my mate."

ACKNOWLEDGMENTS

Sitting down to write an acknowledgment page is much like making an acceptance speech at an award's show. It's more than likely that you will forget someone and then have to spend hours on the phone apologizing for the misstep. And God help you, if it's your mother. So, I should probably get that one out of the way first, right? I need to acknowledge my parents, especially my mother, who have supported me and define the phrase unconditional love. I also want to thank my niblings. They'll eventually be in charge of Silver Orb Books (and responsible for what home I go to eventually). Not sure a mention in the acknowledgments helps, but it's worth covering all bases, right?

First, I need to acknowledge all the readers. Without them, Bray and Vixen would never have watched over (and tried to help) as their pack found mates.

It goes without saying, but I will say it again. Much gratitude to Cassandra. If any of you are shocked and surprised that you didn't have to wait for Broken Witch, that's all Cassandra's doing.

Chan, she's a pillar of unconditional support and a reminder that I am not a complete and total hack when the insecurity hits and I spiral into the dreaded impostor syndrome.

Finally, and of course not least, the wonderful individuals who are responsible for the creation of the collector's edition of the Broken Peak Pack Omnibus: Kasey S., Sherry M., Meg M., Pyndan, Erin C., Rhel, Kieran, Rafael P, Sarah, and Melanie B. Little did they know that by supporting one little Kickstarter, they'd find a permanent spot on my acknowledgments page.

ABOUT THE AUTHOR

Jules Crisare loves writing sexy shifter romances. The growly and dominant males of Broken Peak and the Silver Sentinels are the ones bending to the strong wills of the smart heroines who cross their paths. Seriously, only strong heroines need apply to capture the hearts of these sexy alphas. Get your shifter loving fingers ready to turn those pages and explore the world of the Sentinels of the Silver Orb.

www.JCrisare.com